GIRL ON THE RUN

A job in a patent law firm is a far cry from the glamorous existence of a pop star's girlfriend. But it's just what Jane Porter needs to distance herself from her cheating ex and the ensuing press furore. In a new city with a new look, Jane sets about rebuilding her confidence — something she intends to do alone. That is, until she meets patent lawyer Marshall Winfield. But with the paparazzi still hot on Jane's heels, and an office troublemaker hell-bent on making things difficult, can they find happiness together?

RHODA BAXTER

GIRL ON
THE RUN

Complete and Unabridged

LINFORD
Leicester

First published in Great Britain in 2014 by
Choc Lit Limited
Surrey

First Linford Edition
published 2019
by arrangement with
Choc Lit Limited
Surrey

A catalogue record for this book is available
from the British Library.

ISBN 978–1–4448–4163–3

LP

Published by
F. A. Thorpe (Publishing)
Anstey, Leicestershire

Set by Words & Graphics Ltd.
Anstey, Leicestershire
Printed and bound in Great Britain by
T. J. International Ltd., Padstow, Cornwall

This book is printed on acid-free paper

To my parents.

Acknowledgements

Thank you to Jen Hicks for forcing me to write when I couldn't be bothered, to the lovely folk at Choc Lit for their new edition and gorgeous cover and, of course, to my family without whom none of this would have been possible.

1

CAUSE CELEB: The Magazine that connects YOU to the Stars!

BEDHOPPERS!

In a shock revelation this week, *Triphoppers'* star Ashby Thornton has split up with his long term girlfriend, Jane Porter. Jane, 25, discovered Ashby, 25, in bed with Janelle Shawn, 19, who will be appearing in *Hollyoaks* next month.

After six years together, the separation was bound to be difficult. 'Jane's devastated,' said a friend. 'She and Ashby have been together since they were just students at uni. She stood by him and supported him throughout his career. She doesn't deserve this.'

Sources close to the couple say that this may be a row that they cannot recover from. There have been increasing suggestions of tension between them as Ashby's sky-rocketing career has made his lifestyle ever more hectic, whilst Jane is attempting to build a career in the pharmaceutical industry. 'The pressures of Ashby's social life have been taking a toll on Jane,' said a source. 'She goes to all the important functions with him and still manages to turn up for work the next day. It's not an easy lifestyle to sustain.'

No one has seen Jane since she stormed out of the flat she shares with Ashby. Friends suggest that she has gone into hiding in order to mend her broken heart. Meanwhile, bad boy Ashby has declined to comment.

What do you think Jane should do?

Write in and tell us, or log on to our **website.** Turn to page seven for an exclusive interview with Janelle Shawn — 'How Ashby Thornton sweet-talked me into bed!'

★ ★ ★

It was rush hour on Fleet Street. Jane walked briskly, not out of choice, but to avoid being mowed down by other people. She would have preferred to slow down and look at the buildings she was passing. Perhaps even enjoy the knowledge that she was walking on Fleet Street as someone who belonged there, not just a tourist. Being in London was still a thrill. Even though she loved Manchester, it didn't have the same buzz as London did.

She paused to glance at her watch and was tutted at by a woman in a hurry to get to her desk. Jane tried to apologise, but the woman was already gone, scurrying away with her head down against the watery winter sun.

A bus drove past, featuring a huge advert for the new *Triphoppers'* album on the side of it. Out of habit, Jane ducked her head into her scarf so her face was less visible. Seeing an alleyway ahead, she made a quick dart and stepped out of the main flow. No one took any notice of her.

She relaxed a little and paused to get her bearings. The office wasn't far and she was going to be ridiculously early for her first day as a trainee patent attorney in a large London firm.

She had always wanted to work in London. She might have got there earlier, after she'd emerged from university with a chemistry degree and a determination to never set foot in a lab again. But by then she'd met Ashby and hadn't wanted to be separated from him.

Ashby.

The thought of him still stung, but now that her anger had subsided, she missed him. Or maybe she missed

4

having a boyfriend. It was better to be single and lonely than to have a boyfriend who was cheating on you. Wasn't it?

She let out a long breath. A future without Ashby would have been unthinkable a few months ago, but now that was what she was hoping for. There would be no more music industry parties. No more gigs to shadow him to. No more intrusive pictures in the gossip magazines. She could concentrate on her career. Ashby's betrayal might be the best thing that could have happened to her.

A look at her A-Z showed her that the alleyway would bring her out close to where she needed to be. The road ahead was tarmacked, but narrow. The loading bays and doorways on either side would have made the alley menacing, if it weren't for the fact that there were other people around. Not a huge stream like on the main road outside, but a few people plodding along, not making eye contact. Feeling happier at this pace, Jane carried on.

It was intriguing how people made a conscious effort not to notice each other. As far as she was concerned, this situation was bliss. She wondered how many of these people dreamed of being famous. She had felt like that once, but being at the centre of media attention was not as much fun as people seemed to think.

It had been ages since she'd left Manchester, but the feeling of being stalked by photographers, gossip columnists and the public had still not gone away. Since moving to London, she had tried not to go out unless she absolutely had to, even though the chances of someone recognising her without Ashby were slim.

When she emerged from the alley, the January sun glinted off the windows of a pub, turning it into a mirror. She stopped to straighten her jacket. It took her a few moments to recognise herself. Until last week she'd been blonde and glossy. Now, in her sharp business suit and with dark hair, she looked every inch the lawyer. She gave herself an encouraging smile. A stray wisp of hair flew across her face. She tethered it behind one ear as she rejoined the flow of people, and stepped straight into the path of a runner. His shoulder rammed into her, throwing her off balance. She staggered backwards.

The runner stopped and turned. As he approached, she felt a moment of fear. Was there such a thing as jogger rage? She drew a deep breath and prepared to defend herself.

'Are you OK?' he pulled his earphones out as he approached her.

'Um . . . yes.' She rubbed her arm where he'd bumped into her. It would probably bruise. 'I'm fine.'

'I'm really sorry,' he said. 'You stepped into my path, I didn't have time to — '

Jane held up a hand. 'It was my fault.' She looked up at him for the first time.

His face was shiny with sweat and his hair was tucked under a beanie hat.

Even under such unflattering conditions, it was a handsome face.

'Really,' Jane said with a smile. 'I'm fine.'

'Well, if you're sure . . . '

He gave her a quick smile. A dimple appeared briefly on his right cheek. It was definitely a handsome face. 'OK then.' He turned and set off again.

'Have a nice day,' Jane shouted after him.

He slowed and looked over his shoulder. She had a brief impression of brown eyes before he nodded his acknowledgement and picked up the pace. Without really thinking about it, she checked out his legs. Long. Muscular. Nice.

It had been a long time since she'd been able to admire any man other than Ashby. Maybe moving to London was just what she'd needed. She rechecked the address on her paper and carried on walking with a renewed sense of hope.

★   ★   ★

From: Stevie Winfield, To: Marshall
Winfield
Morning Marsh. Are you in this
evening? Can I call you? Love Stevie.
PS: Have you got an exciting day
planned?

From: Marshall, To: Stevie
I'm a patent agent. Patent agents don't
have exciting days. As it happens, I'm
not in this evening. Why? How much
do you want? M.

From: Stevie, To: Marshall
I'm affronted! Can't a girl call her big
brother without it being about
money?! More importantly though
— you're going out this evening!
What's the special occasion? Have you
got a date? OK, you got me. It is about
money. I need to get the car inspected
. . . love Stevie.

From: Marshall, To: Stevie
No. No date. There's a new trainee
starting in our group today, so we're

all going to the pub after work to get to know her. I don't really want to, but I have to, in case Keith turns it into a 'Marshall is anti-social' thing. He's trying his best to undermine me before the partners' meeting. Why do I have to pay for your car to be inspected? What happened to your allowance? M.

From: Stevie, To: Marshall
Ooooh. A girl trainee! There's hope. There's hope.

From: Marshall, To: Stevie
I have work to do. M.

* * *

The offices of Ramsdean and Tooze were a mixture of open plan desks and glass-fronted rooms. Jane was shown into a small office with two desks facing each other. At one sat a petite girl with a neat bob and square glasses.

She looked up and smiled. 'Hi,' she

10

said. 'I'm Ruth.'

Jane put down her handbag and attempted an easy, confident smile. 'I'm Jane.'

'I know,' said Ruth. 'We had an email telling us about you.'

'Really? What did it say?' The minute she said it, Jane wished she hadn't. The question had come out too eager.

'That you used to work for a pharmaceutical company . . . ' Ruth looked at her intently. 'Why? Were you expecting there to be something more?'

'Oh, no. Just wondered, that's all.'

Ruth's eyes rested on her a little longer. 'OK. I'm supposed to be your buddy for the first couple of days. Would you like me to give you a tour of the office?'

Ruth chatted as she showed her around the building. The office adjoining theirs was empty. Next to it was a desk where a woman with short grey hair and dangly earrings was frowning at her computer screen. 'This is Val,' said Ruth. 'She keeps this place running smoothly.'

Val looked up over the rim of her glasses, and gave Jane a warm smile. 'If only. I can help you with any secretarial support though.'

Ruth indicated the empty office next door. 'Where's Marsh?'

'Meeting,' said Val. 'Poor boy had to run off almost as soon as he got in.'

'You'll meet him soon enough, I guess,' she said to Jane. 'Since Susan's not in today and Marsh is busy, I suppose I should take you to meet Keith.'

'He's in,' said Val, not meeting Jane's eye. 'I saw him a few minutes ago.'

There was a pause. Ruth and Val exchanged a glance. Jane waited for an explanation, but received none.

'Come on,' said Ruth, starting off. 'It's a shame you didn't get to meet Marsh. He's nice. You'll like him.'

Did that mean she wouldn't like Keith?

'Keith's one of the partners,' Ruth

said in hushed tones before she knocked on a door on the other side of the building. 'I often have to work with him.'

When Ruth pushed the door open, the man at the desk looked up from his work. 'What is it?'

'I'm showing Jane round the office.' Ruth let Jane go in ahead of her.

Keith scanned Jane from head to toe and back again, his gaze resting fractionally longer on her legs than anywhere else. His demeanour changed from slightly irritated to all charm. 'Ah. Jane.' He stood, tall and broad in a rugby player sort of way. 'Welcome.' When he leaned across the desk to shake her hand, he gave it a small, and unnecessary, squeeze.

Jane resisted the impulse to back away.

'I'd love to chat, but I'm a little tied up at the moment.' Keith gestured to the files on his desk. 'But, I will catch up with you later in the day, I promise.'

'OK,' said Jane and took a step back

towards the door. 'I look forward to it.'

'Oh, me too.' Keith's glance made another dart towards her legs. 'Me too.'

Once they were outside, Ruth said, 'He'll probably suggest a trip to the pub. He usually does.'

'Usually?' Whilst Jane had been to enough parties to satisfy her appetite for the social whirl, it had been a while since she'd been able to go to a pub. It would be a good way to get to know people, she decided. After all, she knew hardly anyone in London.

'Yes, Keith organises a trip to the pub whenever a new . . . person . . . starts.' For a moment Ruth looked as though she was going to say something else, but she seemed to think better of it. Instead she pointed out the small library.

Jane followed her, wondering what it was that had gone unsaid.

$\star$ $\star$ $\star$

By the end of the day, Jane was exhausted. She had been introduced, informed and trained until she felt completely wrung out. She sank into her seat and checked her email. There were messages from her parents and her friend Polly wishing her luck, but nothing else. She relaxed a little. There was nothing even in the spam box from anyone from the press. It looked like she was finally old news. She told herself she should stop worrying quite so much.

Keith knocked on her office door and perched on the edge of her desk before she could respond. 'Since it's nearly home time, I wondered if you fancied coming for a drink?' He cast a quick glance across to Ruth. 'You too Ruth, of course.'

'I can't tonight, thanks.' Ruth's smile didn't show in her eyes. 'Prior plans.'

'Shame.' He turned his attention back to Jane. 'So, how about it, Jane?'

All Jane really wanted to do was to go home and close her eyes. But she managed a smile. 'Sure.'

'Meet you in the lobby in five

minutes. I'll go rally the troops.' He winked at her and hurried off.

Ruth watched him go. 'Have fun.'

Again, Jane had the feeling there was something Ruth was stopping herself from saying.

'You don't like him, do you?' She shut down her computer and picked up her coat.

Ruth made a face. 'Small personality clash, that's all.' She avoided Jane's eye. 'I'm sure he's OK, really.' She clearly didn't want to be drawn into discussing her antipathy towards someone senior to her.

Jane decided to leave it. After all, she would have ample opportunity to get to know more about Keith in the pub.

* * *

Keith and a tall, thin, Scandinavian-looking man were waiting for her.

'This is Eric,' said Keith. 'He works in the regional office. He's come over to see how the real office operates.' He laughed at his own joke.

Eric rolled his eyes. He reached past Keith and shook Jane's hand, holding on to it so that, for a moment, she was afraid he was going to raise it to his lips. 'It's nice to meet you.' He gave her a wide smile.

They walked to the pub where Jane had checked her reflection in the window that morning. The olde-worlde feel of the exterior was misleading. There were chrome stools at the bar, a scattering of low tables and sofas with puffy cushions further back.

Keith bought a round of drinks and ushered her over to a table surrounded by chairs in fluorescent upholstery. 'So Jane,' he said. 'How're you finding it so far?'

'It's only my first day, but it seems like a nice place to work.'

Keith laughed. 'I meant London. Must be a bit different from up North.' He said 'up North' as though it were a contagious disease.

Jane felt her smile tighten. 'Yes,' she

said. 'It's very different. The air's dirtier, for a start.'

Eric guffawed. 'That's very good.'

Keith stared at her for a moment, then gave an unconvincing laugh. 'Right. That's very funny.'

'Keith here thinks that anything outside of London is the third world,' said Eric.

Jane smiled politely. She'd only been in this man's company for a few minutes and already the anti-Northerner digs had started. This could be an interesting evening.

2

From: James Edwards
To: Marshall Winfield
Pub time! Jim.

From: Marshall, To: James
I'm just writing up the notes from the meeting. You go ahead. I'll join you there. Marsh.

From: James, To: Marshall
No way. You're not wriggling out of it by pretending you're working. I'll be round in five minutes. We can't leave the poor girl to Keith and Eric. They'll schmooze her to death. Besides Lou says I can have the night off. It's pay-back for her going out and leaving me with the kids last week. I can't waste it! Jim.

From: Marshall, To: James
OK. OK. Fine. I'll meet you by the
lifts in five minutes.

*   *   *

Jane shifted uncomfortably in her seat.
Keith was sitting next to her and, not
very subtly, looking at her legs. He and
Eric had been trading insults and
joking, which would have been enter-
taining, if Keith hadn't been showing
Jane so much non-professional interest.
Being arm-candy for Ashby meant she
was used to being ogled at, but she'd
never learned to be comfortable with
the experience. She wondered how
early she could make her excuses and
leave without looking antisocial.

Ordinarily, she didn't mind being
surrounded by men. Before *Triphoppers* became famous, she had spent
many an evening in the pub with Ashby
and the band without feeling awkward.
But then she had been a student and
the band had been just a bunch of guys

her boyfriend sang with. She hadn't needed to impress them.

With these men, the situation was different. They were work colleagues and part of the city set. She could sense undercurrents of professional tension, but didn't know what they were. She felt as though she was a fresher at university once more, aware that allegiances formed and impressions made in the first week would dog her for the rest of her time there. As despondency started to creep over her, she told herself that she shouldn't rush to judge. She took a sip of her wine.

Keith was good-looking enough, but the way he was eyeing her up was irritating. Eric was telling a joke, watching Jane out of the corner of his eye. She recognised that look too, from when she was with Ashby. It was that of someone calculating how useful she would be to them. In her past life, she would have clung to Ashby and played the dumb blonde, but she couldn't do that here. She had to work with these people. She had to show them that she was smart, capable and likeable.

Besides, she reminded herself, she wasn't blonde any more.

'Hallo, hallo.' A cheery voice made them all look up as a red-haired man approached. 'I'm Jim, one of the junior partners.' He had a friendly face and an infectious smile.

Jane liked him immediately.

'Hi.' She wondered if everyone defined themselves by their level of seniority in the company.

Jim moved aside a little. 'This is Marshall. One of the associates.'

He was tall and handsome and looked oddly familiar. She hadn't been introduced to him at the office, she would have remembered. And she didn't know many people in London. Where had she met him?

'Hello again.' Marshall's brown eyes lit up. A dimple appeared in his cheek.

The jogger from that morning! He looked different in a suit and with his hair neatly combed. She had thought that underneath the sweat and the jogging clothes, he might be quite attractive. It turned out she'd been right.

'Oh! I didn't recognise you . . . ' She was about to say 'with clothes on' but realised how inappropriate that would sound. She felt her cheeks warm.

Marshall seemed to sense the rest of the sentence and his smile widened.

'Do you know each other?' Keith's eyes narrowed as he looked from one to the other.

'Yes, we ran into each other earlier this morning. Literally.' Marshall looked around. 'Can I get anyone a drink?'

'I'll have a pint of the usual,' said Jim. 'I'll grab us a couple of seats.'

Keith moved his stool slightly closer to Jane. Jim dragged a stool over and sat on the other side of her. 'So,' he said as he shrugged off his coat. 'How was your first day, Jane?'

'It was good, thanks.' Jane waited for

any comparisons to life in the North, but none came.

Marshall returned and sat opposite Jane. By then Keith was talking again. There was a certain over-the-top quality to the way Keith spoke, as though he was trying to project more personality than he actually had. Jane tried to listen to him, but found her attention kept being drawn towards Marshall. He really was very handsome. But then, Ashby had been handsome. It didn't mean he was a nice person.

When there was a lull in Keith's monologue, Marshall said, 'So, Jane, what made you decide to become a patent agent?'

Jane had been asked the same question at almost every job interview. 'I wanted to be involved with cutting edge science without actually doing any lab work. I figured, what better way than to become a patent attorney and help people file patents to protect their brilliant inventions.'

'Too right,' said Jim. 'Leave the

research to people who are good at it, I say.'

Marshall shot Jim an amused look and turned his attention back to Jane. 'You started off working in the pharmaceutical industry, right?'

Jane wondered if he'd been reading her CV, or whether that information had been part of the email that Ruth mentioned.

'So why did you decide to leave Manchester and come down here to move into private practice?'

Jane decided to ignore the first part of the question; it would be impossible to explain her reasons for leaving Manchester without mentioning Ashby. 'I wanted to work on a wider variety of projects.' She made eye contact with Marshall for the first time and immediately forgot what she was about to say.

There was a brief pause and she realised that everyone was watching her. Reluctantly, she looked away from Marshall's eyes, only to find herself looking at his lips. Hurriedly, she focused on the safer territory of his eyes again. 'How about you? Did you always work in private practice?'

Before Marsh could answer, Keith said, 'Marsh has always been with R and T.' He clapped Marshall on the shoulder. 'Started off as a mere trainee.'

Marshall raised his eyebrows at Jane and nodded. 'What he said.'

Jim laughed. 'Marsh is one of our bright young things,' he said. 'Who knows, he might make it to partner one of these days.'

Keith gave a derisive snort.

'I worked as a research chemist for a bit before I came here,' said Marshall. 'As you say, the variety appeals.'

The arrival of Jim and Marshall had changed the tone of the evening. Jim's good humour was infectious and the conversation moved swiftly away from work to teasing Eric about his upcoming wedding. Jane noticed that Marshall didn't say a lot. She wondered if that meant he was shy. Keith had stopped looking at her legs quite so often and was using the time to make supercilious remarks, mostly aimed at Marshall. Marshall, whilst not openly ignoring Keith, appeared not to hear any of them.

Jane found the interaction between the men amusing. After her second glass of wine, she found she was fighting the urge to giggle. For the first time in a long time, she relaxed and was surprised to realise she was enjoying herself.

★   ★   ★

It was late by the time Jane returned to the flat. Polly was lying on the sofa reading.

She looked up from her magazine. 'Hiya. How was the pub?' Moving to London had taken the edge off Polly's accent, but it was still noticeably from Lancashire. Jane found it comforting to come home to.

She shrugged off her coat and sank

gratefully into a chair. 'Not bad.' She eased her feet out of her shoes. 'I seem to be in a mostly male team.'

'Oh aye? Anyone nice?'

'Well, there's Keith, who was definitely eyeing me up. A guy called Eric who was a bit creepy.' Jane counted them off her fingers. 'Jim, who's lovely, but married and Marshall, who's a bit quiet.'

'Huh. No one promising then?'

Jane stared thoughtfully at her toes. 'Marshall seemed all right.'

Polly peered at her. 'You're blushing.' She leaned forward. 'So, this Marshall. Tell me about him.'

'I ran into him earlier in the morning. Or rather, he ran into me. I stepped out without looking and he was jogging past and ran smack into me.'

'And then you met him again in the pub?'

'It looks like we might be working together sometimes.'

Polly nodded. 'Is he fit?'

Jane felt her cheeks warm again.

'Well, yes. In a Matthew McConaughey kind of way.'

'What?' Polly sat up. 'Dimples?'

'Only one.'

'Oooh. And?'

'And nothing.' Jane decided not to mention that she'd got a good look at him in his running shorts. There were some details best kept away from Polly. 'He seems very nice. But like I said, very quiet.'

'Maybe he's shy.'

Jane laughed. 'Don't get excited Pol. He's a work colleague. He's bound to have a girlfriend anyway. Most nice men our age do.'

'You mean you didn't find out if he was single? Jane, you disappoint me.'

'Pol . . . '

'This is the first guy you've noticed since you got here. I'm allowed to get a *leetle* bit excited.' She held up a finger and thumb to show how little. 'If nothing else, it shows that you're coming out of the depressed state you'd got yourself into.'

'I wasn't depressed, I was angry. I still am.' She sighed. 'I don't think I'm ready to meet anyone just yet anyway. I mean, my last relationship was a total car crash, I'm not really looking forward to going into another one.'

Polly clicked her tongue sympathetically. 'You shouldn't let it get to you. Ashby's not worth it.'

Jane held up her hand. 'I really, really don't want to talk about it right now.'

Polly gave her a long look. 'Fair enough. But if you do . . . '

Jane looked at Polly fondly. They had known each other since they were at school and Polly had always been there for her. When Jane discovered Ashby's infidelity, the first person she'd told was Polly.

'You've done so much for me already,' Jane said. 'I mean, if you hadn't offered me a place to stay so I could apply for jobs here, I'd still be living with Mum and putting up with people whispering about me behind my back.'

Polly waved her hand. 'Don't be silly. It's fun having you here. Besides, what are friends for?'

Impulsively, Jane reached over and gave Polly a hug. 'You're the best, you know that. As soon as Ashby coughs up my share of the deposit from the flat, I'll get out of your hair, I promise.'

Polly laughed. 'Have you had your tea?'

'I don't really feel like eating. I'm bushed.' She pushed her hair back and again was surprised to find it so short. The new haircut was lovely, but she missed having hair long enough to flick over her shoulder.

'At least the new look is working. No one seemed to recognise me. It's nice not having to watch for the press all the time.' Jane stood up and stretched. 'Let's hope they've lost interest in Ashby and his pathetic little life.'

Polly looked at the magazine in her hand. 'Actually . . . '

Jane froze. 'What?'

Polly flicked the copy of *Spotted!* to a

page in the middle and handed it to her with an apologetic wince.

'Oh no. What's he done now?' The magazine article showed Ashby, looking tanned and gorgeous, with his arms around two girls in bikinis. Jane felt her heart contract at the sight of him. He looked well, and happy, without her. Both the girls were draped on him, sporting super white smiles — and she couldn't help noticing — better toned bodies than hers.

She skimmed the text.

SPOTTED! EXCLUSIVE: Pictures of Ashby Thornton with not one, but TWO bikini-clad bombshells.

We have red hot pictures of *Trip-hoppers'* star Ashby Thornton on the beach in Cannes with two blondes, reputed to be sisters. Two months ago Ashby, 25, split up with his long term girlfriend Jane Porter after Jane caught him in bed with Janelle Shawn from *Hollyoaks*.

Ashby is celebrating his newfound singledom whilst on location in France. Sexy Jane meanwhile, is said to be heartbroken and has left Manchester.

Below it was a picture of Jane herself, all sleek blonde hair and make-up, accompanying Ashby to a launch party. The caption said 'Jane, disappeared?'

'Shit.' Jane sank back down into the chair. 'Shit. Shit.' She waved the magazine. 'Why do they have to keep going on about me? Bad enough Ashby's tart goes to the papers about his sordid one night stand.'

She threw the magazine on the floor and buried her head in her hands. 'We could have had a nice dignified split if it wasn't for that. Why does he have to keep dragging me into these things?'

Polly slid off the couch and put her arms around Jane. 'Oh honey. It's OK.'

'But why me? He's got some new bimbos, why do they have to bother with me?'

'Well, maybe it's because you photograph so beautifully.' She held up the magazine. 'I mean look at you. You look like a movie star and you're not even trying.'

'It's all in the make-up. I don't look like that in real life.'

'Especially not now. I think you're worrying about nothing. No one's going to recognise you with your new hair and new image.' Polly gave Jane another hug. 'Besides, no one is going to think of looking for you in a patent law firm.'

That was true. 'I suppose you're right.'

'Of course I'm right.' Polly stood up. 'It'll be fine. Trust me.'

3

www.triphoppers.com

Introducing the Official Triphoppers website — your one stop hotline to the guys in Triphoppers!!

NEW: Download the single 'Dangerous' for free!
Listen to exclusive interviews with the band!
Preview new releases before they hit the shops!
Keep up with Ashby, Pete, Lee and Josh on the official *Triphoppers'* blog.
Free downloads, wallpapers, screensavers, e-cards and much, much more!
Win two tickets to a *Triphoppers'* concert and the chance to meet your heroes in our exclusive

competition!! Just vote for your favourite band member.

Click on their photo below to register your vote.

Ashby — singer, songwriter and all round sex god!

Pete — drummer, songwriter and the Thinking Woman's eye candy!

Lee — lead guitarist and bad boy!

Josh — guitarist, backing vocals and the buffest body in the band!

They're all fantastic, but who is the best? Vote now.

* * *

From: James, To: Marshall
Subject: Jane
She's nice. Did I detect a spark of interest between you? You seemed to know each other from before . . . Jim.

From: Marshall, To: James
Subject: Re: Jane
Like I said, I bumped into her in the street when I was jogging in yesterday

morning, that's all. She's a work colleague. It's never a good idea to mix business with pleasure. You can't have forgotten what happened the last time I did that! And yes, she is nice.

From: James, To: Marshall
Subject: Re: Jane
And pretty too. Do you remember every person you meet in the street? I think not. I suspect you might have some competition from Keith.

From: Marshall, To: James
Subject: Re: Jane
I get the impression I'm not popular with Keith at the moment. I'm not entirely sure how I've managed to piss him off this time. I guess I have to keep him sweet, at least until after the next partners' meeting. I've worked too hard to miss out on a partnership just because I can't stand Keith. Re: Jane. I literally ran into her. Nearly mowed her down. She wasn't looking where she was going and stepped into

my path. So, it's not surprising I remember her. Get off my case. Are you allowed to look at other women? I'm sure Lou wouldn't approve. M.

From: James, To: Marshall
Subject: Re: Jane
Keith's problem is that he's über competitive. It's almost like a reflex with him. He can't seem to help himself. I guess it comes from having super powerful parents. Anyway, he was the youngest person to be made partner in this firm. If you make it this time round, you'll be a whole year younger than he was. He doesn't want to lose his crown. He's a devious one. And clever. I'd watch my back if I were you. Jim. PS: I'm married. Not blind.

From: Stevie, To: Marshall
So? How was last night? What's the new girl trainee like? Stevie.

From: Marshall, To: Stevie
It's 9 a.m. What are you doing online

at this hour? You don't normally get up before 11. The new trainee — Jane — is OK. Seems nice . . . and quite bright. Which is good since she's going to be working on this big opposition case that Susan's got. We're going to need all the help we can get. Marsh.

From: Stevie, To: Marshall
That's not a description. What does she look like? Or did you stare at your pint and not look at her all night? I'm up because I drove Buzz to the station this morning. There didn't seem much point going back to bed afterwards. Besides, I was hoping this new girl might be The One for you. Kisses, Stevie.

From: Marshall, To: Stevie
Why is everyone obsessed with Jane? The poor girl's only been here five minutes and everyone's trying to set her up already. By the way, I'll sort out the money you wanted

this evening. Which reminds me, you didn't answer my question. What happened to your allowance? Marsh.

From: Stevie, To: Marshall
I lent Buzz some money to pay for his trip. Don't worry; he's going to pay me back. I think you're being cagey. Sounds like you like this girl. Did Jim go out with you last night? Stevie.

From: Marshall, To: Stevie
Buzz hasn't paid you back for the last lot of money he borrowed off you, has he? Marsh.

From: Stevie, To: James
Were you out with Marsh and Co last night?? Is there any gossip I should know about? I asked Marsh, but he's being suspiciously cagey about it. How are Lou and the kids? I haven't seen Molly and the twins since I babysat last summer. They must have

grown lots. Is Molly walking yet?
Stevie. X

From: James, To: Stevie
Hi Stevie, Jane — Northern, but not
scarily so. Slim, tall, fantastic legs.
Brown hair. Charming smile. She
seemed to know Marsh from somewhere before. He says they just
bumped into each other in the street.
A likely story. From what I could see,
he couldn't take his eyes off her. She
kept looking at him too, but that
might just be her trying to avoid looking at Keith. Molly's a toddler now.
Photo attached — taken two weeks
ago. Twins started big school a few
months ago! Jim.

From: Stevie, To: James
OMG Molly is ADORABLE! I'm definitely going to have to come and
visit. I hope she remembers me.
Thanks for the goss. I thought my
brother was being cagey. I'll work on
him. Stevie. XXX

41

From: James, To: Stevie
Cheap babysitting is always welcome.
And yes, do keep me posted about
the Marsh situation. Lou often says
it's a tragedy he's still single.

From: Marshall, To: James
Stop emailing my sister nonsense.
Haven't you got better things to do?

4

Ashby Thornton's ex, sexy Jane Porter has disappeared amidst rumours that she is still devastated about the *Triphoppers'* star's betrayal. Ashby and Jane met when they were at university and, according to friends, Jane helped Ashby with his career.

'Without Jane, he would never have made it to where he is now. It's shocking how badly he treated her. She's very upset,' said a close friend.

So upset, in fact, that she's gone to ground completely. Rumour has it that she may even have left

Manchester in order to get away from her painful memories of her time with Ashby.

'It can't be easy,' another friend said. 'What with Ashby's new album being released and posters for his next tour going up all over town.'

We say, Jane, wherever you are, he's not worth it!

★   ★   ★

Jane joined Ruth in the social area for lunch the next day. The room was large and well lit, with round tables and a few well-placed plants making it look a little less corporate.

'We used to have a toaster,' said Ruth as she took her bowl of soup out of the microwave. 'But it was deemed a health and safety risk. I miss making toasties.'

'At least you have a microwave. We didn't even have that where I used to work.' Jane looked around the room. 'Where do you want to sit?'

'I normally sit there.' Ruth pointed. 'With the other trainees.'

'Right.' Jane trailed after Ruth, wondering if even lunchtimes fed into the hierarchy. Ruth introduced everyone to Jane, who forgot their names a minute later. She noticed, as she looked around the room, that most people from Susan's team were there, including Keith. He was sitting with other associates and partners. He didn't seem to have noticed her.

She didn't see Marshall. 'Does Marsh sit with them at lunchtimes?' She couldn't see him and Keith choosing to spend time together.

'He rarely comes out,' Ruth blew on her hot soup. 'He's a bit of a workaholic.' She paused as if in thought. 'He's been keeping to himself much more since the whole Dominique thing.'

One of the secretaries said, 'Who's this? Marsh? Yeah. Dominique was an idiot. I mean, the other guy was nothing special was he? Marsh is way better looking.'

Everyone laughed. 'Seriously,' the girl continued in a low voice. 'Have you seen him in his running shorts? There's no way I'd let that go.'

'You'd have to catch him first,' said another secretary. 'We saw you trying to lure him under the mistletoe at the Christmas do.'

'Oh yes,' said the first girl with a grin. 'And I'll try again this year. Only this time, I'll make sure we're both drunk.' Everyone laughed again.

Jane wondered what Marshall would think. Ashby, she knew, would have thrived on the attention. The thought brought with it a stab of sadness. She sighed and bit into her sandwich.

The conversation turned to gossip about people she didn't know. She allowed her attention to wander, idly looking round the room. Over Ruth's shoulder she could see the table where Keith was sitting. A woman joined them just then. Out of a shopping bag, she pulled out a sandwich and a copy of *Spotted!*

Jane's mouth went dry. Patent attorneys were supposed to have a good eye for detail. Supposing one of them saw her photo and recognised her. She began fiddling with her newly brown hair, until she caught herself and lowered her hand.

When Keith said something, the woman with the magazine turned to listen to him, with one hand idly flicking through the pages. Suddenly she stopped and looked closely at something in the magazine.

Jane tried to look inconspicuous, focusing on her sandwich. A quick glance showed her that Keith and another man were now looking at the magazine over the woman's shoulder.

Jane wondered if she could sneak out, or whether doing so would only draw more attention to her. While she was debating with herself, the woman looked straight at her.

So much for anonymity. She would

have liked to have had a few days to let people get to know her as herself, before her past came crashing in. Maybe even build up some loyalty so that they wouldn't tell the press where she was.

She stood up, gathered up her sandwich, which she no longer wanted, and left as quietly as she could. Behind her she heard someone say, 'Yeah, I reckon that's her all right.'

Back in her office, it took Jane a few minutes to compose herself. At least Ruth wasn't back yet. She was surprised at how awful she felt. Even in this new setting, the idea of being photographed and talked about wrung her out. She tried to pull herself together, but her eyes filled with tears.

Right now, she needed a friend more than ever.

* * *

From: Jane Porter, To: Polly Hartwell
One of the patent attorneys was reading *Spotted!* There isn't a chance it's

a new edition and doesn't have my photo in it, is there? Jane.

From: Polly, To: Jane
It's not time for another *Spotted!* magazine to print, so this one will have your photo in it. It's quite a nice photo of you, if it helps. For someone who appears in these celeb magazines on a regular-ish basis, you are remark-ably clueless about them. Pol.

From: Jane, To: Polly
I'm not a celebrity. I only went to these events because Ashby wanted a bit of moral support and some totty on his arm for his grand entrance. At least that's what he told me. He probably just wanted someone sober enough to get him home in one piece, really. I'm pretty sure they recognised me from the photo. So much for my plan to get on with my life. Bugger. Jane.

From: Polly, To: Jane
Perhaps it won't make any difference.

These people are professionals, after all. Maybe they'll just judge you on your ability to do the job and not take any notice of who you used to go out with.

From: Jane, To: Polly
That would be nice, but I doubt it. You should have seen the excitement when they spotted the photo. They were all crowded round it gawping. I left. I couldn't bear it. It's just horrible. I don't want to spend my life with people watching my every move again. What am I going to do?

From: Polly, To: Jane
Oh Jane. I don't think there's anything you CAN do. You're just going to have to tough it out. It might not be as bad as you think.

★　★　★

Ruth returned to the office before Jane could reply. She quickly closed down her email and blinked back residual tears.

Ruth sat down and started pounding on her keyboard. Her eyes were sparkling.

Jane braced herself for questions, but none came. Was Ruth staying silent out of politeness? As the minutes ticked by, Jane felt her nerves stretching more and more taut. Finally, unable to bear the suspense, she decided to face the questions. 'What did it say?'

Ruth looked up. 'Pardon?'

'The magazine. What did it say?'

'Oh.' Ruth looked furtive. 'Push the door to, will you?'

Jane felt a prickle of hope. She pushed the door closed, as requested.

'There's this girl. Dominique ... ' Ruth began.

Relief washed through Jane, making her body suddenly feel light. It wasn't her they'd seen in the magazine. It was someone else.

Oh thank God.

* * *

From: Stevie, To: Marshall
I see Dominique's made it into the gossip mags — or at least someone who looks very much like her has. She's going out with some footballer, apparently. Have you seen it? Are you OK? Stevie.

From: Marshall, To: Stevie
One of the other attorneys has very kindly left the magazine on my desk for me. Although I'm not sure exactly why she thought I'd like to study a photo of my ex draped over some footballer! Dominique and I split up ages ago. Why should I care who she decides to snog? Marsh.

* * *

Jane had been working at Ramsdean and Tooze for a week and she still couldn't get over the fact that she lived in London now. Normally, she liked to ride on the top deck of the bus, well above the familiar shop displays, where the buildings revealed their true nature. While the shop facades were soulless and modern, the second floors of the buildings displayed styles and decorations that spoke of what they used to be. She found it fascinating.

She hadn't managed to catch a double decker bus that day, so she was at street level. At least she had a seat by the window, so she could watch the streams of people on the streets. What was it about London crowds that fascinated her so much?

It wasn't the diversity of races and colours. Manchester had that, although to a lesser degree. Nor was it the sheer number of people. Partly, she realised, it was what they were wearing. Classic, grunge, traditional garb from various countries and some outfits that were just plain wacky. In the North people tended to dress more uniformly, especially on a winter night.

Jane had tottered to clubs wearing

open-toed high heels and a small dress under her huge coat. She had never been comfortable in the tiny scraps of clothing that most women went clubbing in. After Ashby became famous she had opted for slightly more expensive, longer dresses for media events, earning her the reputation of 'classy bird' among the other band members.

The bus crawled along in the slow traffic and drew up at a bus stop. There was a large advert on the side of the bus shelter. Jane found herself staring straight at Ashby. It was a nice photo, airbrushed slightly to get rid of the acne scars on his cheeks. He stood in the foreground, looking moodily at the camera, with the band fanned out behind him. His light brown hair had been highlighted to make it shine and the camera had caught the lucent blue of his eyes perfectly. He looked younger than he was. And very sexy.

Jane instinctively ducked, hiding her face, until she remembered that she was in London where it was very unlikely anyone would recognise her. As the bus moved on, she risked a glance around. No one paid her any attention. She relaxed and turned back to the window.

When people had first started noticing Ashby and his friends, it had been exciting. They would be doing something fairly normal when giggling schoolgirls would ask Ashby for his autograph. They would ask him what it was like being on TV. Ashby's brooding good looks and the dry wit of the drummer had made them local celebrities.

After a few appearances on TV, they had been offered a recording contract and had acquired PR agents. Through carefully orchestrated exposure, the band had risen to fame. Their first album had been nominated for several awards.

Jane, by virtue of being Ashby's girlfriend, found herself going to parties, chatting with minor celebrities and, usually, making sure her very drunk boyfriend got home safely at night.

She had found glamour difficult. She had always worried about her make-up smudging, her hair not staying in place or her dress being tucked in her knickers. Sensible suited her much better.

She looked down at her sensible work clothes. Her fingers tightened round her bag. What was it about her that made her more comfortable thinking about science and talking to scientists or lawyers rather than socialising with pop stars?

Perhaps, she reflected, it was because she didn't really care about the problems of the famous. When they complained about the intrusion of the press, they were always secretly hoping they'd be quoted. She, on the other hand, found the intrusion genuinely unsettling. She had once thought anonymity was the curse of a mundane life. Now, she felt it was a blessing.

*   *   *

The door of Polly's flat opened straight
into an open plan living room. Polly
had tried to divide the space up by
placing the sofa with its back to the
door. The TV was on so Polly was in.
'Hello,' Jane called as she turned to
hang up her coat.

There was a muffled curse and
Polly's head appeared above the back of
the sofa. 'Hi. I didn't expect you home
so soon.' She sounded slightly breathless. Her hair had escaped from its
ponytail and her face was flushed.

Jane heard rustling and a few grunts
and suddenly realised Polly was not
alone on the couch. She felt her face
heat. 'I . . . er . . . I'll just be in my
room for a few minutes.' Grabbing her
bag, she fled, careful not to look at the
sofa.

In the safety of her room, she sank
down onto the bed. Feeling a terrible
urge to listen to what Polly and Andy
— at least, she assumed it was Andy

— were saying, she dug her iPod out of her bag. Unsure about whether it was safe to go out, she changed into jeans and a jumper and sat on her bed.

The bed was really a sofa bed and, open, it took up most of the room. Polly's nursing books were still stacked in a corner, further crowding the room. Jane lay down and thought about the flat she and Ashby had shared. They had moved in together straight after graduating from university. She had got a job working for a pharmaceutical firm as a trainee patent agent. Ashby had drifted from job to job until he and the band were selected to appear on a TV talent show. After that, he stopped pretending to look for work.

They had been really lucky to find a pleasant one bedroom flat they could afford. At first they'd had very basic furniture and mismatched cutlery. Jane remembered the day she'd bought new curtains for the flat, her first purchase towards making the place a home.

After Ashby's rise to fame, Jane had

found the flat a huge source of comfort. It was home. Whatever act Ashby had to put on when they were outside, once they were home, he was the same haphazard, clever man she'd fallen for when she was eighteen. She loved the predictability of it all. The fact that she knew that while she was cooking dinner or cleaning the bathroom, he would be lying on his stomach on the living room floor jotting down song lyrics and tapping out rhythms with the end of his pen.

The flat had been her sanctuary until the day she'd come home with a migraine and found Ashby in bed with a wannabe actress from *Hollyoaks*. She could still see the girl's red, red nails gripping the familiar lines of Ashby's back, still remember her irrational thought that those sheets were clean on that morning. She would never forget the shock in the girl's eyes when she saw Jane.

Ashby had followed her out of the bedroom, pulling on his dressing gown

— which she had bought him — and making excuses, as though there was anything he could say to make him less despicable. Jane had left immediately, not waiting to pick up anything other than her handbag. She had travelled, dry-eyed, for nearly two hours, until she'd arrived at her parents' house near Oldham. The minute her mum opened the front door, her composure had broken, taking with it her heart. She had cried for days.

At the time she'd thought life couldn't get any worse. Later, when her mother persuaded her to go back and talk to Ashby, she had found that his betrayal of her was the talk of Manchester. People whispered behind her back at work. Photographers kept popping up to take photos of her 'looking distraught'. After one particularly bad afternoon, when she'd been trapped in the house because a photographer and a journalist were camped outside, she'd given up.

She took what she could and went

into hiding in London, which was two hundred miles away and big enough to get lost in.

A month later, she was offered a job. Living with Polly was only ever meant to be temporary. As soon as she got her deposit for the flat back from Ashby she would move out.

Jane stared at the ceiling, hemmed in by the closeness of the walls. She closed her eyes and tears started to slide out from under her lashes.

There was a knock on the door. 'Jane?' said Polly. 'Would you like some tea? I've got a pasta bake in the oven.'

'Er . . . yes,' said Jane, feeling it would be churlish to refuse. 'That would be lovely. Thanks.'

'OK,' said Polly. 'We're ready when you are.'

Andy and Polly were already sitting at the table when Jane walked in. Polly dished out a third portion. For a moment, they ate in silence.

'I'm really sorry,' Jane said. 'I didn't think to knock. I wasn't expecting . . . '

'It's OK,' said Polly. 'You live here. You don't have to knock.'

'Mind you,' Andy said. 'It might be an idea — '

Polly nudged him in the ribs.

'I'm so sorry,' Jane repeated. 'As soon as I get paid, I'll move out. OK.'

'You don't have to,' said Polly. 'I like having you here.'

Andy shot Polly a glance. Polly raised her eyebrows at him.

Jane started to apologise again, but Andy stopped her. 'Forget it, Jane. Really. It's no big deal. You take your time.' He gave Polly a fond look and patted her on the arm. 'It'll probably do us good to learn some self-control.'

Jane looked at them and felt a spark of envy. They were so happy together. Andy might not be the most good-looking of men, but he would never cheat on Polly. She found she'd suddenly lost her appetite, and moved the pasta around on her plate, resisting the urge to push the whole thing away.

'So,' said Andy, breaking the awkward silence, 'what are you doing at work then, Jane?'

'She's looking for prior art,' said Polly, who had asked the same question the night before.

'Oh aye? What's that when it's at home?' Andy spoke through a mouthful of pasta.

'You know what a patent is?'

'Like on *Dragon's Den?*'

Jane smiled. 'Yes, a bit like that. Now, if you're going to get a patent for an invention, it has to be new, right?'

'Sounds fair,' said Andy.

'So, if it's published somewhere before the patent was filed, then it can't be new.' She paused to see if he was following her.

He nodded and waved his fork, indicating that she should go on.

'We're trying to show that a patent shouldn't have been granted. I'm trying to find something that was published before the date the patent was filed, so that I can say that the invention isn't new.'

'OK,' said Andy. 'So where does art come into it?'

'That's just the technical term for published stuff,' Polly said.

Andy looked at Jane for confirmation. She shrugged. 'Not quite, but close enough.'

Andy was thoughtful for a moment. 'Doesn't sound very lawyer-y to me.'

Jane laughed. 'I'm doing the easy bits. Marshall's doing the difficult bit where you have to put the arguments together.'

Polly leaned closer to Andy and said in a theatrical whisper, 'Marshall's the one she fancies.'

Jane shook her head. 'I don't.'

5

The meeting reminder pinged on Jane's computer and she felt excitement rise. She was meeting Susan, her boss, for the first time. Until now, she had been doing odd pieces of work that people found for her and getting to know the company's systems. She was looking forward to having a solid project to work on.

Ruth looked up. 'Meeting?'

'Yes. With Susan.'

'Good luck,' said Ruth. 'Susan is . . . a challenge.'

'People keep saying that. What's wrong with her?'

Ruth frowned. 'There's nothing wrong with her . . . as such. She's just a little brusque, if you see what I mean.'

Jane shook her head.

'Not very hot on people skills. She's

very clever. One of the cleverest attorneys we've got. But she has no patience with people who can't keep up.'

'OK,' said Jane, hoping she would be able to keep up. 'I'll bear that in mind.'

'You'll be fine,' said Ruth.

Jane wished she felt as confident.

★ ★ ★

From: Eric Korsky
To: Keith Durridge
Subject: The new girl.
She seems nice. Do I take it she's caught your interest? As you say, she is very pretty. And has very nice legs.

From: Keith, To: Eric
Subject: Re: The new girl.
She does indeed have fabulous legs. I bet I can get those wrapped round me by the end of the month. K.

From: Eric, To: Keith
Subject: Re: The new girl.

Yeah, yeah, you say that every time a nice looking girl starts. You have no chance with this one my friend. She's way out of your league. And, as you've let your prejudices against the provinces show, you've probably blown it already. Very proud folk, these Northerners, you know. E.

From: Keith, To: Eric
Subject: Re: The new girl.
Bet you a £100. K.

From: Eric, To: Keith
Subject: Re: The new girl.
I'm not playing that game any more. I'm a happily engaged man now, remember? Besides, I haven't forgotten how much trouble it got us into last year.

From: Keith, To: Eric
Subject: Re: The new girl.
I'm not suggesting you compete with me. We all know you couldn't anyway. Just a little sportsman's bet.

I'll even set a time limit for my success. One month. I'm getting bored out of my mind around here, I could do with a challenge. Go on, live a little.

From: Eric, To: Keith
Subject: Re: The new girl.
You don't stand a chance. If the undercurrents at the pub were anything to go by, she's more likely to be interested in Marshall Winfield than you. We all remember what happened the last time you went after a woman who had her eye on Marshall Winfield.

From: Keith, To: Eric
Subject: Re: The new girl.
Yes, well Dominique wasn't exactly a normal woman. There's no challenge in getting off with a nymphomaniac. Winfield is welcome to her. Now Jane, on the other hand, seems like a very classy, if slightly repressed, woman. One who has standards. The

only reason Winfield even got a look in was because I hadn't turned on my legendary charm.

From: Eric, To: Keith
Subject: Re: The new girl.
Since you insist, I shall take you up on this. £100 plus dinner at the club. And you only have until the end of the month. I shall enjoy watching you crash and burn.

From: Keith, To: Eric
Subject: Re: The new girl.
You're on, Korsky. Prepare to pay up. K — the man.

*   *   *

The meeting room had wide windows overlooking the Thames. Far below tourist barges crawled up and down the water. The millennium wheel moved lazily in the distance. Since she was early, Jane took the opportunity to spot landmarks.

Someone cleared his throat, making her jump. She spun around to find Marshall at the doorway, a cup of coffee in one hand and a clutch of files in the other.

'Good morning,' he said as he put down his files. 'It's a good view from up here. We've all got so used to it, we take it for granted.'

'I was just looking to see if you can see the Tate Modern.'

'Oh you can. You have to sort of lean into the window though.' His eyes were so brown they made her think of chocolate.

Jane suddenly felt like a teenager. Her heart sped up and her mind went blank, just when she needed a witty comment.

Keith sauntered in. 'It must be quite exciting for you, coming from the provinces.'

Marshall's shoulders tensed.

'Manchester,' she said, 'is hardly the provinces. It's the Northern capital.'

'Exactly.' Keith pulled out a chair

next to her. 'The Northern capital. It's nothing like the real capital, is it?' He laughed, as though his comment were hilarious. 'I've been here all my life,' he said, serious again. 'I'll show you around one weekend, if you'd like. There's more to London than meets the eye.'

Was he coming on to her? She was saved from having to come up with a retort when Susan walked into the room.

Susan wore a perfectly cut suit with tottering high heels and her make-up had an American gloss to it. Blonde hair framed her face in soft ringlets. Only the lines by her eyes suggested she was in her forties. Both Keith and Marshall seemed to straighten up slightly, as though coming to attention.

Susan looked at Jane, her face expressionless. She held out her hand. 'I'm Susan,' she said, speaking very fast. 'You must be Jane.'

Jane stood up clumsily and took the proffered hand. 'Hi.'

'I'm sorry I wasn't there to meet you on your first week.' Susan gave Jane's hand a firm shake. 'I hope you enjoy working with us.' She sat down and took a Mont Blanc pen out of her jacket pocket. 'OK, let's get started. What have we got?'

Marshall opened his mouth to speak, but Keith jumped in before him. 'I've been going through Marsh's searches and some that I did myself,' he said. 'I haven't found a piece of killer prior art yet, but I think we might have a few angles that we can attack from.'

Susan indicated he should go on. Jane leaned forward on her elbows and tried to follow the conversation. As far as she could tell their client was trying to attack two patents. One for a novel drug and one for the combination of that drug with an already known one. Keith was researching ways of attacking the first and Marshall was working on the second.

The sun came out from behind a cloud, casting Jane and Keith's shadows on the table. Marshall put his hand up to shield his eyes. Susan clicked her tongue impatiently and said 'Jane, can you draw the blinds please?'

'Thanks,' Marshall said when she returned to her seat. Slivers of light still fell on his face and hair, making him glow slightly. The sight of him did something strange to Jane's knees. She sank back in her chair and turned her head so that she was looking at Susan instead.

As Susan and Keith continued their discussion, Jane found she couldn't follow it. Her eyes kept drifting towards Marshall. She told herself sternly that she had only just started work there. This was no time to get involved in an office romance.

When Keith had finished speaking, Susan turned to Marshall, who gave her a concise report of his research. She listened without comment until he'd finished, then fired questions at him. Marshall responded, making several suggestions for future research. Jane listened carefully to the exchange and took note of things she needed to research further.

'OK,' said Susan, when Marshall had finished. 'Sounds like we're making progress.' She tapped a finger on the table. 'Now then, Jane. How's your database searching?'

Jane jumped, and began, 'I haven't — '

'Good, good.' Susan stood up. 'You can help Marshall with his prior art search. He'll teach you the basics. You seem pretty bright. I'm sure you'll pick it up.'

Jane nodded, in what she hoped was a confident and enthusiastic manner.

'Actually,' said Keith, 'I could use some extra help evaluating these papers.'

Susan turned to him. 'Didn't you say Robert was working on it?'

'Well yes,' said Keith. 'But it's a lot of work. I'm sure Marshall can spare Jane from time to t — '

'I'm sure Robert can manage.' Susan

nodded to Marshall. 'Set up another meeting in a week's time. I'm seeing the client in nine days' time and I want something to show them.'

Without any further pleasantries, Susan left the room.

Keith shot Marshall an angry glare. Marshall ignored him. The hostility between the two men was palpable.

As Jane stood up to leave, Keith said, 'I guess it's going to be a busy week for all of us.' He flashed Jane a smile. 'Welcome to the team.'

★　★　★

From: Marshall, To: James
What is Keith's problem? Susan told Jane to work with me on my case and Keith looked like I'd stolen his lolly.

From: James, To: Marshall
Don't mind Keith. He's just jealous. First Susan gives you equal weight to him on this case, then assigns the latest totty to work with you. Result:

Not only do you get an extra pair of hands to work with. They belong to a lovely young lady. Lucky boy.

From: Marshall, To: James
Will you stop it. You can get done for sexual harassment for saying stuff like that.

From: James, To: Marshall
Ah come off it. I saw you looking at her in the pub. I haven't seen that gleam in your beady little eye since — well, a bloody long time. Lou thinks you should go for it, by the way.

From: Marshall, To: James
Haven't you and Lou got better things to talk about than my love life? Jane's lovely, but I think I'll stay out of it for a while. I think Keith's got his eye on her anyway. I don't really want to antagonise him any more than I have to. Besides, office relationships aren't a great idea. Not for me anyhow.

From: James, To: Marshall
Mate, we've got three kids. Your love life is the most exciting news going as far as we're concerned. At least it doesn't have anything to do with the kids. Anyway, Jane's just walked past, so I'm guessing she's heading to your office. Be good. If you can't be good, be careful. Jim.

★ ★ ★

Marshall jumped when Jane knocked on his office door. He turned around 'Hi.'

'Is this a good time?' she said. 'You were going to show me the search databases.'

'Right. Yes, just a second.' He rummaged in a desk drawer and pulled out a notebook.

'Passwords,' he explained. 'Shall we go to your desk? That way you can get to work straight away.'

Jane led the way back to her office.

'May I?' Marshall leaned on the desk

and took her mouse. 'This is the website.' He had to lean across her to type in the URL. He smelled faintly of soap and aftershave. 'I'll just bookmark it for you.'

Jane was suddenly very aware of how broad his shoulders were. She tried to concentrate as he pointed to the screen and explained what various parts of the website did. His fingernails were short and clean. He had long fingers. She liked men with long fingers. Ashby had had long fingers . . .

'Does that all make sense?'

Jane looked up to find Marsh regarding her quizzically, his face quite close to hers. Close enough to touch. Or kiss. He blinked and straightened up.

Jane felt herself blush. Were her thoughts that transparent? 'Yes. I think I've got that.'

She ran through it again, just to make sure. He moved back a step so he was at a less intimate distance.

'If you have any problems, just come

find me.' He gave her a smile, without making eye contact, and left.

Jane stared after him, her face still hot with embarrassment. What was wrong with her? Marsh was attractive, sure, but she should be able to talk to him without turning into a quivering wreck. She was acting like a love-struck teenager. She doubted she'd been that nervous around men even as a teenager. Not even with Ashby.

Ruth's voice cut into Jane's thoughts. 'I shouldn't bother, if I were you.'

She had been so distracted by Marsh that she had completely failed to notice Ruth, sitting quietly at her desk. 'Pardon?'

'Marsh,' said Ruth. 'I saw the way you were looking at him. I shouldn't bother. I mean, he's a total sweetie and everything, but he doesn't date people in the office.'

Jane stared at her. 'I don't . . . '

Ruth grinned. 'Don't worry. It happens all the time when new girls start. Most of the secretaries fancy him.

He's a lovely guy, but he doesn't really date much. And even then, not people from the office.'

Before Jane could say anything, Ruth continued. 'He did date one of the trainee patent agents once — a girl called Dominique, the one that was in *Spotted!*, but it all went a bit wrong and they split up. Things were quite awkward for a while. Then she left.'

Jane didn't want to be having this conversation, but she couldn't help herself. 'What happened?'

Ruth glanced at the door and leaned forward. 'She and Marsh were an item, for a while,' she whispered. 'Then, this 'friend' of hers turned up to visit her from America. No one thought anything of it, but apparently, he was more than just a friend, if you know what I mean. Anyway, Marsh found out and dumped her.'

Having been through something similar herself, Jane felt a pang of sympathy for Marshall, especially as the details of his humiliation seemed to be common knowledge. 'How come you know about it?'

'Dominique wasn't really the discreet type . . . she was pretty upset when Marsh split up with her and kept going into his office and making a scene and saying it didn't mean anything. Everyone heard . . . ' Ruth pulled a face. 'In the end the partners had a word with her and she left.'

Jane stared. 'They sacked her?'

'Not sacked, exactly. Just encouraged her to leave.'

Jane was about to ask more questions, when Ruth's phone rang. She gave an apologetic glance and answered it, leaving Jane to stare at her screen, digesting what she had just heard.

*   *   *

From: Stevie, To: Marshall
Erm, Marsh, can you send me the car inspection money, please? It's getting quite urgent . . . Love Stevie.

From: Marshall, To: Stevie
Shouldn't you ask Buzz to pay it?
After all, he owes you a lot more than
that.

From: Stevie, To: Marshall
Geez. It's only a hundred quid. You'd
think it was YOUR money!

From: Marshall, To: Stevie
It IS my money. I'm not letting you use
your trust fund to subsidise your boyfriend. What are you going to do if he
leaves you, having borrowed most of
your cash? Honestly, Stevie. I know
you think he's perfect right now, but
can you really be sure? I mean, he's
borrowed money from you three times
in the past two months and hasn't
paid you back. Doesn't that suggest he
doesn't ever intend to? M.

From: Stevie, To: Marshall
You know, your problem is that you
don't trust people. Just because Dominique hurt you, doesn't mean

everyone is out to get you. Look, I need to get the car inspected. I can't afford to pay it any other way. So, will you give me the money or not? S.

From: Marshall, To: Stevie
Fine. I'll LEND you the money. I would like you to pay me back within two months. Marsh.
PS: This has nothing to do with Dominique.

From: Stevie, To: Marshall
Stop acting like you're Dad. You're not.

6

From: Jeremy and Marjorie Porter
To: Jane Porter
Dear Jane, Ashby called for you. I told him you didn't want to speak to him, like you asked me to. He sounded ever so apologetic and said he was missing you. I think, perhaps you should talk to him. Do you want me to give him Polly's number if he calls again? Love Mum. PS: Dad sends his love.

From: Jane, To: Jeremy and Marjorie Porter
NO! DO NOT give him Polly's phone number. Mum, he was having sex with another woman in our bed. There is no way on earth that we're going to get back together. And I do not want to speak to him ever again. Jane.

From: Mike Taylor
To: Ashby, Pete, Lee, Josh
Guys. We're all set for launching the new album in three weeks' time. The publicity campaign is ready to go too. We're going to try and market Ashby, rather than just the band. If I can get one of the gossip mags to pick it up, we could go viral, which would be fantastic. Mike.

Cause Celeb Blog: The magazine that links YOU to the stars!

Pining for Jane

He's a star. He's young, he's handsome, he could have any girl he wants. But Ashby Thornton — inset — looks miserable. He was snapped leaving his local pub alone and looking unhappy. Since splitting up with his girlfriend of four years, Jane Porter, he has dated a string of nubile young beauties, but clearly none of them have made him happy. Has Ashby realised that there's more to life than glitter?

★ ★ ★

From: Eric, To: Keith
I see Marshall's got the new girl working with him. Bad luck buddy. Looks like dinner is on you! Eric.

From: Eric Korsky, To: Indra Somasundara
Indra, please book my usual table at the club for me and Keith D. Sometime next month. Please coordinate with my diary, as always. Eric.

From: Keith, To: Eric
I still have until the end of the month. It ain't over till the fat lady sings. Or, in this case, the thin lady. Keith.

From: Polly, To: Jane
Hi. Andy's coming over this evening

and we're getting pizza. Want to join us? Pol.

From: Jane, To: Polly
Nah. You and Andy need to have some quality time together. I'm thinking of doing a bit of extra work before I come home tonight. I've still got to finish going through the latest search to get a list of documents that I need to read. I should be home around nine. Do you want me to text when I get to the tube station? ;-) Jane.

From: Polly, To: Jane Porter
Stop it, you're making me blush. No warning necessary. I'm sure we can be respectably eating pizza by nine. Pol.

★   ★   ★

Jane pushed the pile of paper away and ran a hand over her eyes. She had been reading the lists of patents for several hours, pausing to print the interesting looking ones off the web. Ruth had gone home an hour or so before. There were only two days left before they had to meet Susan and she had failed to find anything of use. With the deadline looming, she and Marsh had split the remaining patents between them and were both reading as fast as they could.

There was a knock on the office door. Jane swung her chair round and saw Keith leaning with one arm against the door frame.

'Hi,' he said. 'Working late, I see.'

'Yes.' She stretched her arms out in front of her to get rid of the stiffness. 'Although I don't think I can read another word.'

'I know what you mean. Do you fancy a post work drink?'

She was too tired to do any more work. It would be an hour before she could go home. She really didn't want to walk round the shops now. A quick drink would fill in the time nicely, even if it was with Keith. 'Sure. Why not.'

'Great. I'll meet you at the lifts in ten?'

When Keith had left, Jane wondered if she'd made a mistake. She would much rather have gone for a drink with Marsh. She looked thoughtfully at the wall between their offices. He might want to join them. She wouldn't be alone with Keith, and she could get to know Marsh a bit better outside of work.

She could no longer pretend that she didn't fancy him. Every time he walked into the room she had to fight hard to concentrate on what she was doing and not stare at him. She did her best not to be alone with him, which was difficult, considering they were working together and she had to have daily update meetings with him.

Trying to ignore her attraction to Marsh hadn't worked. Maybe she should at least find out if he was single. At any rate, it was good to get to know one's work colleagues.

Besides, she wouldn't be alone with

him. Keith would be there. She hurried round to his office, before she talked herself out of it.

Marsh was reading at his desk, his fingers massaging his temples. He looked up with a tired smile when she knocked. 'Find anything?'

'No, sorry. We're going out for a drink before heading home. Do you want to join us?'

He glanced back to the pile of paper on his desk. 'I've still got to finish this lot . . . ' As he spoke, he stifled a yawn. 'Oh what the hell,' he said. 'I'll take it home and read it there. Just give me a minute to tidy up.'

* * *

From: Keith, To: Eric
Am just heading out for a drink with the lovely Jane. Prepare to pay up Korsky. The bet is as good as won.

* * *

Jane returned to Marsh's office, bundled up against the cold. He was pulling on his own coat. He'd left his bag on his desk and she pointed it out.

'I'm running home,' he said. 'I'll come back and get changed before I head off.'

'Running? In this weather?' she said as she followed him out. 'Won't you freeze?'

'Not if I'm running.' He held a door open for her. 'You said 'we', I should have asked who else was going for this drink?' As he said it, they walked out into the lobby. 'Oh, hello Keith.'

'Winfield.' Keith's face darkened.

'I thought I'd invite Marsh along . . . ' said Jane. It suddenly occurred to her that Keith and Marsh might not have wanted to spend time in the pub together. She chided herself for being so stupid.

The look of annoyance on Keith's face was swiftly replaced by a more neutral expression. 'Excellent. The more the merrier. After all, we're all part of the same team, right?'

The lift arrived, saving anyone from having to answer.

* * *

The bar was crowded and noisy, so loud that they had to shout to be heard. Jane was wedged between Keith and Marsh. Once they'd hollered a few banalities about the weather and a few comments about work, the conversation dried up and they stood in a group, sipping their drinks.

After about half an hour of trying, and failing, to have a conversation, Marsh looked from Jane to Keith and back again, as though dealing with some sort of internal conflict. He seemed to come to a decision and sighed. 'I'll see you tomorrow,' he shouted, leaning in close so she could hear him. She could feel the warmth of his breath.

She lowered her head to hide the blush she knew was colouring her cheeks.

As Marsh shouldered his way out, Keith moved fractionally closer, his arm pressing against hers. 'So, tell me about yourself, Jane. What did you do before you came to London?'

Jane tried to carry on with the shouted conversation, but her heart wasn't in it. All she could think about was that Marsh had left. Clearly he wasn't interested in her.

After a few moments, Keith suggested they move on to a quieter pub.

Jane checked her watch. 'Oh no. I have to go. I promised my housemate I'd . . . do some stuff for her.' She moved away before he could object.

He followed her out. 'I'll walk you to the tube.'

Jane didn't really want to spend any more time with him. The magnitude of her disappointment when Marsh left had surprised and upset her. She had thought she just had a small crush on him, but now she felt there was more to her feelings than that. Surely, she couldn't be falling for someone so soon after her breakup with Ashby? A four-year relationship must take longer than a few months to get over.

'Actually, I'm going the other way. I'll see you tomorrow.' She turned and walked back towards the office. After a few yards, she checked to see if he was following and was relieved to see he wasn't.

The city was eerie at that time of night. Aside from the odd person hurrying home and the islands of light and sound around the pubs, the streets were empty. The little alleys and byways between buildings that made London such a joy to explore in the daytime became black holes along which the cold wind blew.

As she passed her office building, Jane paused and looked up at the floor she worked on. There were lights still on. She wondered if Marsh was still in there, getting his things and changing into his running gear. She could go up and speak to him. But then, what would she say? What excuse would she have for returning? Shaking her head, she walked on.

She was acting like a schoolgirl with a crush. This wasn't like her. Without thinking about it, she turned into the small alleyway next to the pub that led out into Fleet Street.

Her footsteps echoed in the dark alleyway. She caught a waft of something smoky and acrid. More than just tobacco. Her senses snapped back to the present. Ahead of her a bright spark glowed and then expanded to show a shadowed face.

'Hello, darlin'.'

She stumbled backwards and heard a snigger behind her. A quick glance over her shoulder showed a dark silhouette against the mouth of the alley.

Fear tightened her throat so that the scream hovering there came out little more than a squeak.

'There now,' the man with the cigarette said. 'No one's about to hear you.'

He stepped towards her.

Jane frantically tried to remember what she'd learned in a long-ago self-defence class. She shrank back, into the hands of the man behind her.

'Hey!' The shout was accompanied by running footsteps. The man holding Jane swore. He shoved her to the ground and the other one snatched her handbag. They fled as the footsteps came closer.

Jane huddled on the icy ground, unable to move.

Her saviour came to a stop beside her, panting. She stole a peek and saw a dark, hooded figure, barely visible in the weak light. It bent towards her.

'Are you OK?'

His voice was familiar. Her terrified mind refused to put a label on it.

Jane attempted to sit up. 'I think so. Just a bit . . . shaken.' He helped her get to her feet. 'They took my bag,' she said, still dazed.

'Can you walk? It might be wise to get into the light.'

The unspoken words 'in case they

come back' sprang to the forefront of her mind. She followed him towards the end of the alley, walking slowly, still too dazed to think properly.

'Are you sure you're all right?'

She looked up and this time she recognised his voice. 'Marsh?'

'Jane?'

'Marsh.' She went limp with relief. 'Thank goodness.'

He led her to the main road and along to a bus stop, his arm half-supporting her. Her legs were still too wobbly to support her entirely, so she sank onto a prop seat. Only then did she really see Marsh. He was dressed in a hoodie and running shorts. He must have been on his way home.

He pushed back his hood. 'Did they do anything to you?'

Jane shook her head. 'They stole my bag.'

'That's no big deal. So long as you're not hurt.'

'Thank you. I'm glad you came along.'

Marsh made a small sound. 'I was leaving the office when I saw you go into the alley. I came this way, to make sure you were OK. If I had known it was you, I'd have caught up sooner. What on earth were you doing down a dark alley anyway? It's safer going the long way round.'

'I guess I wasn't concentrating.' She couldn't very well say she had been thinking about him. She knew she had been very lucky. If Marsh hadn't been leaving the office at exactly the right time . . . The realisation of what could have happened hit her and she started to shake.

Marsh put a hand on her arm. 'I think you're in shock. Let's get you somewhere warm.' He looked around. 'There's nowhere near here . . . apart from work.'

'No. Not work.'

'I'll call a taxi and take you home.'

Jane thought of the flat, with Polly and Andy and the millions of questions she'd have to face. 'No,' she said weakly. 'Not there either.'

Jane thought of her flat that she'd had to give up. She thought of the photographer that had waited outside to catch her when she and Ashby had split up. She wanted to go home. Not to Polly's flat, but home. Somewhere she could just hide from the world and sleep. Tears filled her eyes.

'Tell you what,' said Marsh after a moment's silence. 'Why don't we go to my place? I'll make you a nice cup of tea and you can phone the police from there.'

That wasn't home either, but the idea appealed. Jane wiped her eyes with the back of her hand and looked up at him.

'No funny business,' he said, putting his hands up in front of him. 'I promise.'

She didn't doubt that he meant it. So she nodded.

He pulled a mobile out of his hoodie pocket and made the call.

7

Marsh was still in his running shorts. Even bundled up in several layers of clothing, Jane was still feeling cold. He must have been freezing. The taxi pulled up at what looked like an old school in a quiet side street.

Marsh led her into the house and up what seemed like endless stairs. On the third floor, he opened one of the doors leading off the landing and stepped aside to let Jane enter.

As he went round, flicking on lights, Jane stared. Despite the building's Victorian exterior, the flat was very modern. The room had a high ceiling and enormous windows down one side. The décor was warm reds and creamy yellows. Marsh hurried around the room, scooping up items that had been left lying around.

Jane watched him, bemused.

'I wasn't expecting visitors.' He dropped everything into a drawer under the coffee table. 'Take a seat. I'll put the kettle on.'

The flat didn't look like a bachelor pad. There were photos on the walls and floral cushions on the sofa. She did see evidence of Marsh living there, though. A pile of paper and patent books was stacked on the dining table, a jumper was thrown over the back of a chair and a full set of *Buffy the Vampire Slayer* DVDs sat on a shelf.

Jane pulled a bar stool up to the small breakfast bar that separated the kitchen area from the dining table. Against the wall were one haphazardly balanced stack of mountain biking and running magazines and, behind it, a neat pile of *Cosmo*. Jane stared at it. What kind of a man read *Cosmo*?

Marsh saw her looking at them. 'Oh, they're not mine. They're Stevie's. You should report your mugging to the police. You'll need a crime number for cancelling your credit cards.'

She would need to remember what had been in her bag. 'Have you got a piece of paper? And a pen?'

He went back to making tea whilst she tried to remember all her purse had contained.

'Here you go.' He set a mug of tea in front of her. 'I'm sure I had some biscuits,' he said, as he opened one cupboard after another. 'Ah, here we are.' He pulled down a packet of digestives and put them in front of her as well. 'Now, will you be OK for a few minutes?'

'Yes, sure.' She wrapped her hands round the mug of tea, immediately feeling a little better. She smiled at him.

'In that case, I'll just go and get changed into something warmer.'

'Would it be OK if I phoned my flatmate. She'll be wondering where I am.'

'Of course. Phone whoever you want to.' He gave a quick smile and left the room.

Jane waited until she heard another

door close and quickly punched in Polly's number, thankful that she knew it by heart. 'Hi Pol, it's me,' she said when Polly answered.

'Jane, where are you? I've been trying to call you, but you didn't answer your phone. I was starting to get worried.'

'I'm fine,' said Jane. 'My phone got nicked . . . '

'What? How?'

'I . . . er . . . I got mugged.' It seemed too weird to say that. Until now, muggings were something that happened to other people, like winning the lottery. It seemed strange to be the victim of one.

'Oh my God! Are you OK? Where are you?'

'I'm fine,' Jane repeated. 'Marsh rescued me.'

'Marsh?' said Pol. 'Is that the one with the nice arse?'

Jane couldn't help but smile. Trust Polly to remember that one fact above all else. 'Yes, that's the one.'

There was some murmuring in the background and Polly said, 'Shut up Andy.' Then, 'So where are you now?'

'I'm in his flat . . . ' Jane felt a strong urge to giggle.

'*What?* Jane, what's going on?'

Suddenly, it was all too funny. 'He's in the shower,' she said, giggling. 'He made me a cup of tea.'

'Jane? *Jane*, you're scaring me. Tell me where you are and we'll come and get you.'

'No, no.' Jane wiped her eyes with the back of her hand and tried to stop the laughter. 'I'm fine. Honestly. Marsh has been a total gentleman. He brought me in here into the warm and made me a cup of tea. He even gave me his phone to call the police and report the mugging.'

There was silence from the other end, and then Polly said, 'Let me get this straight. You got mugged. This guy with the nice arse rescued you and took you back to his flat?'

'Yes.'

'Why didn't he bring you to *your* flat?'

'I asked him not to,' said Jane, suddenly feeling bad. Polly would have looked after her.

'Why?'

Jane didn't want to hurt Polly's feelings by telling her that she didn't really feel at home in her friend's flat. She felt like she was in the way. 'I . . . He was wearing running shorts,' she said finally.

Now it was Polly's turn to laugh. 'OK, I see what you mean. Well, if he tries anything funny, just call me and Andy will come and pick you up, OK?'

'OK.'

'What's the number there, just in case?'

Jane turned the phone round and read the number that was printed on it in neat feminine handwriting. She had seen Marsh's scrawl before. It wasn't his.

She heard the bathroom door open. 'He's coming back. I've got to go,' she said and quickly hung up. She dialled the police and was busy giving the policewoman a list of what was stolen when Marsh came back in. She didn't look up, but concentrated on what she was saying. She could hear him moving around, making himself a drink.

She heaved a sigh of relief when she'd finished.

Marsh leaned on the other side of the breakfast bar. 'Sorted?'

'I think so.' He was barely a foot away from her. His hair was still damp from his shower and stood in unruly ridges where he'd run his fingers through it. She could smell his shampoo. She looked down, afraid to look into his eyes in case he noticed that she fancied him.

'You should cancel your credit cards,' he said, finally.

'Yes, I should.'

'Would you like some food? I could do us some pasta.'

Suddenly her stomach reminded her that she hadn't eaten since lunchtime.

'That would be lovely.'

As she made her phone calls, she watched Marsh cook. If anything, he looked even more sexy in jeans and a long-sleeved T-shirt. He moved confidently round the kitchen, slicing garlic and chopping vegetables.

When he said he'd make pasta, she had assumed he would just open a jar of sauce. She hadn't expected him to cook a proper meal from scratch. She tried to remember the last time a man had cooked for her. Ashby's idea of cooking was making a sandwich.

By the time Jane had finished her calls, the kitchen smelled wonderful. He got plates out. 'Would you like a glass of wine? I'm having one.'

'Yes, please.'

He placed two glasses of red wine and a big dish of pasta with a tomatoey sauce in front of her and pulled up a stool opposite her. 'Cheers,' he said, raising his glass.

Now that the food was in front of her, she found she was really hungry.

Jane tried a bit of her pasta. 'This is delicious,' she said. 'Thank you.'

'You're welcome.'

'To be honest, I was surprised to see you made it from scratch,' said Jane, when she'd eaten a bit. 'Do you cook a lot?'

Marsh thought for a moment. 'I guess I do,' he said, looking surprised. 'I never really thought about it before. I had to make sure Stevie had a healthy diet, so I started to cook for us. I guess I've just got used to it now.'

Stevie. Jane felt her heart sink. Why had she assumed that a man like that would be single? Of course, no one at work had mentioned that he had a girlfriend, only about Dominique, but then, perhaps he kept it quiet. He seemed like a fairly private person and the office was full of gossip. 'Your girlfriend is a really lucky woman.'

Marsh coloured slightly. 'Oh, Stevie's not my girlfriend. I don't have a girlfriend. Stevie's my sister. She lives with me.' He pointed to a framed photo on the wall behind her. 'That's her there.'

It was a photo of a family. Marsh was there, looking a lot younger and, standing next to him, was a small girl.

'Of course, she's a lot older than that now.'

The family resemblance was unmistakable. 'Are those your parents?'

'Yes,' said Marsh. 'That was taken in my second year at uni. It was about a year before the accident.'

'Accident?'

'They . . . they died. In a car accident. When I was twenty-one. Stevie was only thirteen then, so I became her legal guardian.' He was still looking at the photo.

She tried to imagine what it must have been like to lose your parents and suddenly be in charge of a child at the same time. 'Wow. That must have been . . . ' She couldn't think of a word that covered the situation. 'That's tough.'

He looked back at his plate. 'We

managed. Stevie's a great kid. She looked after me about as much as I looked after her.' He turned his attention back to her. 'Enough about me,' he said. 'How about you? How are you getting on at Ramsdean and Tooze?'

'OK, I think,' said Jane, and paused. 'Is everyone obsessed with rank?'

'Oh yes,' Marsh said with a completely straight face. 'You have to introduce yourself stating where you fit in the company hierarchy. I tried not to for a while, but people kept asking me if I was a trainee.' He shrugged. 'It's silly, I know. But you're in that atmosphere for so long every week that you start to think it's normal.'

'You seem to be able to distance yourself, though.' Jane sipped her wine.

'I used to be more immersed,' he said. 'I've had to teach myself to step back every so often since . . . ' He looked embarrassed. 'I . . . er . . . had an intra-office relationship that went a bit wrong. It gave me a crash course in perspective.'

'I heard about that.'

'I thought you might have done. The gossip network at R and T is pretty comprehensive,' he said, sounding a little apologetic. 'Good old Dominique. Gone, but never quite forgotten.'

Jane swirled her wine. She hadn't talked about Ashby to anyone other than her mother and Polly. She hadn't been ready. Somehow the idea of telling Marshall, who had been cheated on himself, seemed easier to contemplate. She avoided looking at him. 'I know what it feels like to have your partner cheat on you,' she said. 'I caught my ex in bed with another woman.' It felt strange saying it out loud. She waited for the pain to hit.

'You actually saw them? Ouch. That must have been nasty.'

For a moment, she'd thought the hurt had gone away, but there it was. Gnawing away at her. Briefly she considered telling Marshall about how much it had hurt to walk in and find Ashby and the stick insect busy on her nice clean sheets. But then, perhaps he knew? The stick insect had given a fairly frank interview about the whole thing. So maybe everyone knew. Did he ever flick through his sister's magazines? If he did, might he connect her with *Triphoppers*? As she paused for too long, she could see Marsh starting to look worried.

'Yeah. It was pretty nasty. But I'm over it now.' Then, feeling a little honesty was required, she added, 'I think.'

Marsh gave her a sympathetic smile. 'It takes a while.'

'It makes you feel really stupid, doesn't it? You wonder what else was going on that you didn't see.'

'And if the whole world knew and it was only you who didn't see it.'

Jane wondered if he knew just how close that was to her own thoughts. 'Yes. And you wonder how you could have been that bad a judge of character.'

They both looked down at their drinks.

'Well, I guess that's something we have in common then.' The dimple appeared briefly in his cheek.

Jane felt the sudden urge to touch it.

He raised his glass, and said, 'To cheating partners. Good riddance.'

Jane had to laugh. 'Good riddance. We're better off without them.'

Marsh laughed too as he lowered his glass.

She wondered what it would be like to kiss him.

Suddenly the phone rang. Jane jumped. Was Polly checking up on her?

Marsh looked at the number and slipped off the stool, mouthing 'excuse me'. He retreated to the other side of the kitchen, still within earshot, but giving the illusion of privacy.

'Yes?' He sounded slightly annoyed. He listened for a moment. 'That's OK. Don't worry about it.'

He listened some more. His face softened. 'You too. Listen, I've got to go. I've got someone visiting.'

He shot a quick glance at Jane. 'Yes.'

There was some babble on the other end. He rolled his eyes. 'I'll email you tomorrow. Bye.' He hung up, smiling. 'My sister,' he said, by way of explanation.

Jane glanced at her watch. It was eleven-thirty and she had to be at work tomorrow. She hesitated, not wanting to bring the evening to an end.

Marsh noticed her checking her watch. 'I guess we should think about getting you home.'

'I still have my Oyster card. It was in my pocket.'

'Oh no, I can't let you take the tube at this time of night. Especially after all that's happened to you this evening.' He reached for the phone. 'I'll call you a taxi.'

Jane opened her mouth to protest. Apart from anything else, she had no money on her.

'I'll pay,' he said, as though he'd read her mind. 'I insist.'

Once Marsh had ordered the taxi, he opened one of the curtains. 'Do you mind if I turn some of the lights out, so that we can see the taxi when it turns up?'

When she shrugged, he turned the dining area lights off and they stood side by side, watching the road below. They chatted about work and London, but Jane could barely concentrate on what she was saying. She was hyper aware of him standing next to her.

He felt so big and warm and safe. She wanted nothing more than to close the small gap between them. His chest was so close she would only have to move a tiny bit to rest her head against it and hear his heart. Just when the temptation was getting unbearable, a taxi turned into the road.

'There it is,' said Marsh, his voice sounding strained. 'We'd best get out there before he beeps and wakes Mrs Watkins on the ground floor.'

As he helped her into her coat, Jane said, 'I never got to say thank you.'

'I didn't do much.'

'No, I don't know what would have happened if you hadn't come along. And dinner . . . was lovely too.' She raised up on her tiptoes and, with her heart hammering in her ears, she kissed him on the cheek, just next to the dimple.

Marsh froze.

For a moment they stood there, their faces millimetres from each other. Jane forgot to breathe. The world seemed to stop still. Suddenly there was a beep from outside.

Marsh looked into her eyes. He placed a light kiss on her cheek. 'No funny business,' he whispered, his breath warm on her skin. 'I promised.'

8

From: Stevie, To: Marshall
What happened? What happened?
What happened?? I hope I didn't
interrupt when I phoned last night.

From: Marshall, To: Stevie
No, you didn't interrupt anything.
We were just talking. What happened? Well, it's a long story. I was
leaving the office to run home and I
saw someone being hassled. So natu-
rally, I ran to see if I could help.
There was a woman being mugged
by two men. I shouted and ran
towards them. They ran away. It
turned out the woman was Jane.
God knows why she decided to use
the shortcut at night. You'd think
she'd know better. She's from
Manchester! Anyhow, she was all
shaken up. I offered to take her

home, but she didn't want to go there. So, I took her to the flat, gave her a cup of tea and some pasta. We were just chatting about stuff and you rang. That's all. Marsh.

From: Stevie, To: Marshall
What do you mean 'that's all'? Didn't you snog her?

From: Marshall, To: Stevie
No, I didn't snog her. I wanted to. But I didn't. It didn't seem right to take advantage when she was all shaken up. That would make me a total shark, wouldn't it? Besides, when I invited her back to the flat, I promised no funny business. M.

From: Stevie, To: Marshall
What did you do that for, you idiot? God, no wonder none of your relationships last more than a month, apart from Dominique the bitch. It's this gallant crap you insist on pulling.

From: Marshall, To: Stevie
And there was me thinking it was
because I lived with my little sister.
Silly me.

From: Stevie, To: Marshall
OK, even if that was the problem,
you have no excuse for the last year
when I've been away at uni?

From: Marshall, To: Stevie
Apart from the whole Dominique
thing? If we exclude that, I have
no excuse. I hang my head with
shame.

From: Stevie, To: Marshall
Wait a minute. A self-deprecating
joke?? You like her! You really, REALLY
like this girl! Which means you are a
super big GIANT idiot for not kissing
her. What am I going to do with you?
I hope you're at least going to ask her
out today. So that you can snog her
without feeling like you're taking
advantage.

From: Marshall, To: Stevie
I'd like to ask her out, but you know how badly things can go wrong when I date people from work. We work in the same team, which means we wouldn't be able to avoid each other. At least with Dominique, she was at the other end of the office. Also, I'm trying to make partner, remember. I've already had one warning about office relationships — cue Dominique again. I can't risk another. Besides, Jane's just come out of a bad relationship. I think she still feels a bit fragile about it. It's probably not a great idea for me to land her with another one.

From: Stevie, To: Marshall
Fine. Fine. Whatever. But you DO like her, don't you?

From: Marshall, To: Stevie
She's pretty. She's clever. She's nice. She's interesting. And I feel totally at ease when I'm talking to her. So yes, I

like her. But she's still a work colleague, so I can't ask her out. Sorry to disappoint you. Marsh — boring old fart. PS: Of course, all this makes it very distracting to work with her.

From: Stevie, To: James, Cc: Louise Edwards
Jim, I think Marsh likes this Jane girl. But he's refusing to ask her out because they work together. Can you talk some sense into him? I'm CC 'ing Lou in case she has any good ideas about it. Stevie.

From: Stevie, To: James
One other question Jim. What's Jane's last name? Stevie.

★   ★   ★

Jane yawned and switched her computer on. It had been a long night and she was still shattered. It had taken a lot of effort to drag herself into work on time.

121

Ruth's head appeared above the partition. 'Late night?'

'Eventful. I had my purse nicked.'

'Oh my god, are you OK?'

Jane decided not to tell the whole story about her and Marsh. 'Yes, I'm OK. Just a bit pissed off. I had to buy a new phone and a new handbag to put it in on the way into work. It's a real pain.'

'If you need to borrow a bit of money to tide you over . . . ' she said.

'That's really kind of you,' said Jane. 'But I think I'll be OK.'

'Well, the offer's there.' Ruth sat back down.

'Thanks.' Jane opened up her email.

* * *

From: Polly, To: Jane
We heard you sneaking in during the small hours last night. So? What happened? I want details. Pol.

From: Jane, To: Polly

122

Nothing much happened. I told you
he rescued me from the muggers.
After that, we went to his flat.
He made me tea and got me to
phone the police. Then he cooked
me dinner. He made pasta sauce
from scratch, Pol. He just got the
ingredients out and cooked. No
fuss. And it was delicious. I didn't
know men could cook like that.
Ash's idea of cooking me dinner was
to make me a tuna sandwich! Marsh
was a total gent the whole time.
We talked. He's so NICE. And so
grown up — especially after Ashby
and his mates! Apparently, Marsh's
parents died when he was twenty-
one and his sister was thirteen.
So he's had to look after his sister
all that time. She's at uni now. She
lives in the flat with him during
the holidays. I found out he was
single, by the way. He's had a
disastrous relationship fairly recently
and has been single ever since :-)?
Jane.

From: Polly, To: Jane
So, did you pull? Are you going to
see each other again?

From: Jane, To: Polly
No, didn't pull. I thought for a
moment that he was going to kiss
me . . . but then he didn't — well,
he kissed me on the cheek, but
I don't think that really counts. He
did promise that he wouldn't try
anything when he first invited me
to his flat. I guess he was keeping
his word. Of course, now all I can
think about is what it would have
been like if he DID actually kiss
me. I have a huge pile of work
to do, but I can't concentrate.
Aaargh!

From: Polly, To: Jane
Hang on, hang on. He's good-looking,
he's charming, he can cook, he's
single. He lives with his sister. AND
HE DIDN'T MAKE A MOVE ON YOU.
Are you sure he's not gay?

From: Jane, To: Polly
NO. At least, I'm pretty sure he's not.
His last relationship was with a
woman in the office . . . And he isn't
camp.

From: Polly, To: Jane
Not all gay men are camp, you know.
There's one sure way to tell. Does he
fold his clothes up neatly, or just
throw them on the floor? Pol.

From: Jane, To: Polly
If I knew the answer to that, we
wouldn't be having this conversation.
I have a plan. I'm going to ask him
out for dinner. To say thank you.

9

From: Marshall, To: James
Help! My life has suddenly gone
wrong. In order of increasing impor-
tance: 1. I have four working days
before I have to give Susan my opposition draft. I've been wracking my
brains to come up with some decent
arguments. I have a few, but no really
good prior art document to hang it
on. The ones I have are, at most,
tenuous. 2. I have three patent drafts
due in by next week. I'm going to
have to phone at least one client and
ask for a time extension. I hate doing
that. It looks really unprofessional. 3.
Stevie's dating some prat who keeps
borrowing money off her. When I try
to tell her so, she gets annoyed with
me. I thought she would have grown
out of the whole 'you're not Dad'
thing by now. 4. Last, but not least, I

really like Jane and I can't ask her out because she's a work colleague. I know Keith is already trying to put the oar in with the partners. I can't give him more ammunition. I'd like to keep away from Jane, but it's a bit difficult when I work with her every day. She's so damn lovely, I can't concentrate on my work. Just shoot me. Marsh.

From: James, To: Marshall
Sounds like a mess all right. Can't help you with the time management issues. I'm sure you'll cope with your usual style. I'll see if Lou has any ideas on how to help with the Stevie situation. Perhaps a quiet woman to girl chat. Regarding Jane . . . How MUCH do you like her? Jim.

From: Marshall, To: James
I like her a LOT! It was all I could do not to kiss her last night. And in a weird way when I'm with her — outside of work, I mean — I feel like

everything is just . . . right. Which is
odd, since I haven't known her very
long. Marsh.

From: James, To: Marshall
Sounds like you've got it bad.
So, ignoring it and getting on with
life isn't an option then? Assuming
the answer is no, why not wait
until after the partners' meeting.
Then ask her out. You'd have to
keep things discreet, obviously. Set a
few ground rules etc. But there's no
reason why it shouldn't work that
way. Jim.

From: Marshall, To: James
That's a good idea. Why didn't I
think of that??

From: James, To: Marshall
Because this love stuff is turning your
brain to cheese. I was like that when I
first met Lou. Luckily, I was a student
back then and didn't need to do
much thinking. Jim.

From: James, To: Marshall
>> *It was all I could do not to kiss her last night.* Hang on, what happened last night? Why did you fail to kiss her? My secretary tells me that Jane got mugged last night. What's going on exactly? Jim.

From: Louise, To: James, Stevie
So, our Marsh has fallen for someone. Hurrah! About time too. From what Jim says, she sounds like a nice girl — not like that bizarre Dominique woman. What did he see in her? Yes, we must persuade him to do something about it. Lou.

From: James, To: Louise, Stevie
Dominique was a force to be reckoned with. Once she set her sights on Marsh, the poor man didn't have a chance. I hate to burst your bubble ladies, but I think Marsh is right about not dating work colleagues. It would be best if he did nothing about it until AFTER the partners'

meeting. He has worked very hard for this company and deserves a bit of recognition. It would be a shame to throw it away because of a girl. Jim.

*   *   *

Jane looked through Marsh's door. He was frowning at a patent and scribbling notes in the margins. She knocked.

He looked up and smiled. 'Come in. How are you feeling today?'

'I'm fine, thanks.' She went in, but didn't sit down.

'What can I do for you?' He looked back to his work, as though anxious to get back to it.

Jane fidgeted with the sleeve of her blouse. 'I wanted to thank you for everything yesterday.'

Marsh waved her thanks away. 'Don't worry about it. It was nothing.'

'No, it wasn't nothing. So . . . can I buy you dinner? To say thank you.'

Marsh appeared taken aback. 'You don't have to do that.'

'I'd like to.'

He appeared to study the paperwork in front of him. 'Um . . . '

He was going to refuse, she could tell. She had been wrong about how he felt and she had been so certain. 'It's no big deal. You don't have to.' She started to back away.

'Oh no.' He looked up again, his eyes flicking to the doorway behind her. He lowered his voice. 'It's just not a good idea to mix work and fun . . . '

Jane could feel that her face was bright red now. 'Right.'

'But,' he said quickly, 'as you say, it's just dinner to say thank you, right?'

Jane held her breath.

'So, that sounds fine. When did you have in mind?'

'How about Friday night?' That way, if things went really badly, they wouldn't see each other until after the weekend.

Marsh pulled his diary towards him and leafed through. 'Um . . . the week after would be better for me. How about Wednesday?'

'Sure. Next Wednesday then. Great.'

'Hang on, I'll just write it in.' He scribbled in the book. 'There, you're in the diary now. So it's official.'

'Well, I'd better get back to work I guess.'

'I'm looking forward to it.' His dimple flashed.

'Me too.'

★　★　★

From: Marshall, To: James
Jane was just in here. SHE asked ME out! She wants to buy me dinner to say thank you for helping her last night. I suggested next Wednesday. The partners meet that day, so by Wednesday night the decision will be made. Marsh.

From: James, To: Marshall
Well done. I don't know how you do it. I've never been asked out by a woman. Ever. Jim.

From: Marshall, To: Stevie
OK, just to let you know. Jane and I
are going out to dinner next week.
She wanted to buy me a meal to say
thank you. Marsh.

From: Stevie, To: Marshall
YAY!!! I'm very excited for you. You'd
better kiss her this time! You'll have
to give me a full report the next day.
OK, maybe not a FULL report. There
are some things I don't need to know
about my big brother. Love Stevie.

*   *   *

Jane stared at her computer screen and
tapped a nail on the edge of the
keyboard. The night before, she had
been convinced that Marshall liked her,
but now she wasn't so sure. His
reluctance to accept her invitation had
surprised and upset her. No wonder he
had been such a gentleman the night
before. It was easy to be chivalrous if
you're not tempted to go any further.

Thank goodness she hadn't thrown herself at him. That would have been terribly embarrassing. The trouble was, she still fancied him and she would have to sit through dinner, knowing he was just being friendly. She just knew she wouldn't be able to stop thinking about kissing him the whole time. It made her warm just thinking about it.

She placed her hand against her cheek. It was a major disadvantage having such pale skin.

*　*　*

From: Jane, To: Polly
Well, I asked him out. He didn't seem all that keen. I'm all embarrassed now.
Jane

From: Polly, To: Jane
Ouch. That doesn't sound good. I bet he's gay.

From: Jane, To: Polly
You're not helping.

* * *

There was a knock on the door. It was Keith. He ignored Ruth and looked at Jane. 'I heard you got mugged. Are you OK?'

Jane frowned. It had been less than half an hour since she'd told Ruth. Gossip travelled really fast in the office.

She didn't want any more attention. 'It wasn't such a big deal. More of a bag snatching, really.'

Had Marsh been telling everyone about how he rescued her? She hadn't thought he would be the sort, but then she'd been wrong about people before.

She had been wrong about Ashby.

'I thought it was more serious than that,' said Keith. 'Mind you, Sally does tend to exaggerate.'

Jane forced a little laugh. 'No. No big deal at all.' She wondered how Sally knew.

'Well, if you need anything, my door is always open.' He turned to leave. 'I'll see you later.'

When Keith had left, Ruth popped her head above the partition. 'I'm sorry. I didn't realise you didn't want people to know. I mentioned it to Val when I gave her my last set of dictation notes. She must have told Sally.'

Jane sighed. Val was Marsh's secretary. Sally was Keith's. If the secretaries were talking about it, then the whole company probably knew by now. The last thing she wanted was people taking an interest in her life again. At least this time they'd be asking her how she was and not talking in hushed whispers when she passed. And there would be no photographers waiting to snap when she was least expecting it.

'It's OK,' she said. 'It really wasn't anything major. Just a bit of hassle to lose my cards and phone. That's all.' At least now she knew it wasn't Marsh telling people about what had happened.

Ruth sank back down into her chair, mouthing 'Sorry' again.

Jane waved the apology aside. She

opened up the file she was working on and got back to work.

★ ★ ★

From: Stevie, To: Marshall
Marsh, I've just Googled your friend Jane. Turns out there's another Jane Porter, from Manchester. That Jane used to go out with Ashby Thornton. Isn't that a weird coincidence? Stevie.

From: Marshall, To: Stevie
Oh, I see what you mean. They do look similar.

From: Marshall, To: Stevie
I did a little digging. Comparing Jane's LinkedIn profile to the various bits of information from articles about Ashby Thornton's girlfriend, it would seem they both went to the same university. It seems too much of a coincidence. So, I think they're the same person, but she seems to have changed her appearance a fair bit. I'm

sure she has a good reason for not wanting to be recognised, though. Best to respect her wishes. M.

From: Stevie, To: Marshall
Does it bother you? The girl you fancy is famous!

From: Marshall, To: Stevie
Why should it bother me that she went out with someone rich and famous and talented? Marsh.

From: Stevie, To: James, Louise
Ok, I Googled Jane. Turns out she's famous. She used to go out with Ashby Thornton. She was all over the magazines when she and Ashby split up. He cheated on her with a girl from *Hollyoaks*. It was a TOTAL scandal. The mags said she'd disappeared. Looks like she reappeared in your office! Wow! Although, I'm worried now. What does a glamorous ex-WAG want with my brother??? Stevie.

From: James Edwards, To: Stevie,
Louise
Who the hell is Ashby Thornton?

From: Louise, To: James, Stevie
Jim, do try and keep up. Ashby
Thornton is a pop singer. He's the
latest thing, according to all the celebrity mags. Stevie, don't worry about
it. Just because Jane used to be in the
public eye, doesn't mean she's going
to hurt Marsh. As for what she sees
him — what are you talking about?
He's gorgeous, he's successful, he
owns his own flat and to top it all
off, he's a lovely man. What's not to
like? Lou.

From: James, To: Louise, Stevie
Oi, wife, I AM reading this you know.
A man doesn't need to hear that his
wife thinks his best mate is gorgeous!
Stevie, from what I've seen of Jane,
she's a nice person and doesn't really
fit the 'glamorous ex-WAG' bill. If she
was that sort of a person, she would

have sold her story to the Daily Mail and made some money out of it. It sounds to me like she's trying to get on with her life. First you worry that he WON'T go out with her, then you worry that he WILL. You women perplex me. Jim.

From: Louise, To: James
Don't worry, darling. You are, were and always will be, the love of my life. What do I need a good-looking man for, when I've got you? Lou.

From: James, To: Louise
Dammit woman, you always win me over with your sweet talk. I love you too. Jim.

10

From: Polly, To: Jane
Where are you? Are you working late
AGAIN? It's no fun watching Desper-
ate Housewives on my own! Pol.

From: Jane, To: Polly
Sorry! We've only got four days until
we have to report to Susan and I
still haven't found anything that
Marsh can use. I've got about thirty
articles to look through in the hope
that one of them has a throwaway
comment about combining drugs.
To make things worse, I can't keep
my mind off Marsh. It's really quiet
at this time of night and the office
walls are so thin that I can hear him
talking into his Dictaphone. Just
knowing that he's so close is driving
me insane. And my head hurts.
Jane.

From: Polly, To: Jane
You're working too hard. That's why
your head hurts. Come home. Have a
glass of wine and watch Desperate
Housewives with me. Pol.

From: Jane, To: Polly
Maybe you're right. I'll go pick up the
last research paper I've printed out
and I'll call it a day. See you in a bit.
Jane.

★　★　★

Jane stood and stretched. Her back was
stiff from sitting still. She rolled her
shoulders, trying to loosen them. The
walk to the shared printer in a room
around the corner would do her good.

The floor was quiet. Everyone else
seemed to have gone home. It seemed
strange to see the place so still, when it
was normally buzzing with people. She
heard a door shut somewhere. So, there
were others working late.

She paused at a window. It was

another cold night and the beginnings of fog were starting to thread through the streetlights down below. She shuddered, and forced herself to look away from the street, up at the other tower blocks. A number of them had lights on here and there.

She ran a hand over her tired eyes. She didn't know which was more depressing, seeing the enormous amount of reading she had to do, or nearing the end of the list and still not finding anything of any use. Once she got home, the last thing she'd want to do was read, so she'd try to read the remaining document on the way.

Jane turned in to the print room and found Marsh kneeling, loading paper into the printer tray.

He looked up and smiled. 'Still here? I thought Keith and I were the only ones mad enough to stay this late.'

'I was just thinking of heading off, actually,' said Jane. 'I'm nearly at the end of the list.'

Marsh pushed the drawer shut,

stood, and dusted off his knees. 'I guess you haven't found anything.' The printer whirred into life.

'Nothing. I've started dreaming about patents.' She sighed. 'I think I'm losing the will to live.'

'I know that feeling,' he said. Printed pages began emerging and falling into a neat pile.

Jane's mind had gone completely blank. When a page shot out of the printer and slid off the top of the pile, they both reached for it.

Marsh's hand grazed hers. An electric thrill ran up her arm. Her breath caught and she looked up, straight into his eyes. The paper fell, unimpeded, to the floor.

Held in his gaze she couldn't move. He was so tantalisingly close.

Marsh drew a breath and blinked. He cleared his throat. 'Sorry,' he murmured.

He picked up the paper. 'I think this is part of yours.' He hesitated, looked at it more closely. 'Looks like it might be relevant.' He sorted through the rest of the printed papers, making two piles. 'These are yours too.'

'Thanks,' she took the pages, careful not to touch him again. What now? Did they walk back to the office together? Did she go first, with him behind her? What?

'I . . . er . . . was just going to get a cup of coffee,' he said, and walked around her to the door.

'Right,' said Jane, relieved. 'I'll see you later then.' She noticed his coffee cup was still sitting on the counter beyond the printer.

'See you later,' he said.

'Right,' she said again, but she doubted he'd heard her. He was nearly running down the hall towards his office.

Jane returned to her office, trying to get her thoughts in order. Once she got there, she looked at the document she'd printed out. She skimmed the front page.

Marsh had been right. It did look

relevant. She came to a halt in front of her desk and, still standing, she started to read.

There it was. Buried in the conclusions was a sentence suggesting that combining two classes of drugs might lead to more effective results. Just the thing she was looking for.

She stared at the paper for a moment. All these hours of wading through patents and research papers and she'd found it. Quickly, she flicked to the front to find out the publication date. She cross checked the date to see if the paper had been published before the patent had been filed. Her heart sank to see that the date was one day after the date she needed.

She was just about to put the paper into the pile of others she'd already read when she caught sight of a small line of text. *Published on the web* and a date that was a full two weeks earlier. Which meant that it had been available to the public for several days before the patent had been filed. So the inventors could have read it before they put the patent in.

She gave a little squeak of excitement. Without stopping to think, she headed towards Marsh's office.

He was at his desk, clearly tidying up to go home. 'What's up?' he said, when she rushed in.

She thrust the paper into his hands. 'Paragraph before last.' She tried not to jiggle up and down with excitement.

A smile crept across his face as he read. 'When was it published?' He flipped to the front and his smile faded. 'It's a day too late.'

Jane leaned across and triumphantly stabbed at the date it was published on the web. 'There!'

Marsh looked where she pointed. 'Fantastic! This is perfect! Jane, you're a genius.'

When he looked up at her, she was still leaning across his desk. Too close.

Her eyes focused on his mouth. If she leaned forward just a little bit, she could kiss him. She knew it wasn't strictly appropriate, but there was no one else in the office. Who would know?

She wasn't sure if he liked her. What if he didn't?

Somewhere in the middle of her next thought, Marsh kissed her.

Her heart stopped for a second and then restarted, hammering hard and fast. She'd been right all along. He wanted her just much as she wanted him. She kissed him back with passion.

Marsh moved around the desk so she was no longer leaning at an awkward angle. He moved his hands to her waist.

Jane ran her fingers through his hair, pulling him closer. Her heart pounded, almost deafening her.

Somewhere a door slammed. They jumped apart. Footsteps sounded in the hallway, coming towards Marsh's office. They stared at each other, with lips parted, both breathing hard.

'Evening,' said Keith. 'I see we're all still here.'

She took one step away from Marsh as she turned to look towards the door.

'What's going on?' Keith said, looking from one to the other.

Jane was sure her cheeks were flaming. She glanced at Marsh, whose lips had clamped into a line. 'I . . . found this paper.' She picked it up. 'I thought it was relevant.'

Keith took the paper and started to read.

Marsh winced.

Jane bit her lip. She wanted, more than anything, for Keith to go away and leave her alone with Marsh. But there was little chance of that.

'Hey, this looks very interesting.' Keith flipped through and looked at the date. 'Bugger. It's a day too late.'

'Is it?' said Marsh. 'What a shame.' He shut down his computer. 'I guess that's me done for the day.'

Jane suddenly realised he hadn't wanted Keith to know about the paper. She wondered why. Surely, they were all on the same team.

'Oh hang on,' said Keith. 'It was published online two weeks earlier. It could still be relevant.'

'Certainly could be.' Whilst Keith read the relevant paragraphs, Marsh continued to pack up.

Jane fidgeted, wishing Keith would leave.

'Well, this is brilliant. Just what we were looking for!' He folded the document in half. 'This calls for a celebration. Let me buy you a drink.'

'I . . . er . . . ' Out of the corner of her eye, Jane could see that Marsh had frozen in the act of putting on his suit jacket. 'That's really nice of you, but I have a terrible headache.' She frowned in what she hoped was a convincing display of pain. 'I was thinking of finishing up here and heading off.'

Keith looked from her to Marsh and back again. 'Actually, it is quite late. I'll walk you to the tube station. We don't want a repeat of yesterday's incident, do we?'

She gave him a weak smile.

'I'll meet you in the foyer in ten minutes.'

Jane couldn't think of any way out. She would have to let Keith walk her to the station. 'I'll see you tomorrow,' she said to Marsh.

'Yes. Have a good evening.' Marsh surprised her with a smile. 'See you tomorrow.'

'Not running today then?' said Keith, as they trooped out of Marsh's office.

Marsh held the door for him. 'I decided I couldn't be bothered.' He looked over his shoulder at Jane and twitched an eyebrow.

She stared at him, not sure what he meant, but he merely smiled and followed Keith out.

Jane returned to her office, confused. She relived Marsh's kiss. Just the memory of it weakened her knees. To her surprise, she realised that she hadn't experienced that melting feeling in years. Not since she'd first got together with Ashby.

At least now she knew that Marsh liked her. But what now? It was only one kiss.

And he'd pretended nothing had happened after Keith walked in. In fact, he had been almost anxious to get away from her.

From what she had heard of Dominique, she wasn't surprised that his previous experience had made him cautious. Without thinking she touched her lips. Was she supposed to pretend it had never happened?

She had no idea where this was going to go. If all else failed, at least they were going out for dinner next week. She was about to email Polly when her phone rang.

'Hello? Jane Porter . . . '

'Jane, it's me,' said Marsh, speaking quickly. 'Just wondered if you wanted me to wait outside for you . . . '

'Yes please,' she said with a smile. 'That would be nice.'

'Do you think you can get down before Keith catches up with you?'

'I'm on my way.'

'Brilliant. See you in a minute.'

Jane ran for the lift, pulling on her

coat and scarf as she went. She glanced anxiously at the glass doors, fearing that Keith would appear and catch her. She watched the numbers, willing the lift to move faster. It arrived at the same moment as Keith walked into reception. He stopped to sign out and didn't appear to have noticed Jane. She leapt into the lift and closed the door before he saw her.

Marsh was standing just outside the building, waiting for her. 'He's right behind me,' she said.

They walked quickly towards Holborn, side by side, but not touching. Marsh wasn't wearing a coat and had his hands stuffed into the pockets of his suit jacket.

'Where are we going?' said Jane, when they stopped on a kerb to wait for a lorry to emerge from an alley.

Marsh looked sideways at her, the streetlight casting his face into shadow. 'My place?'

The lorry was nearly out now. Jane

cleared her throat. 'Um . . . funny business?'

His eyes sparkled in the streetlight. 'Absolutely.'

* ⋆ ⋆

When they emerged from the underground station into the suburban night, it was cold enough for Jane to see her breath, but she felt warm with anticipation. As the train left, Marsh took her hand and his palm burned against hers. They walked faster.

At his apartment building, they practically ran up the stairs. Marsh let go of her hand, so he could open the door, but dropped his keys. For an instant Jane felt a stab of worry that he might be one of those men with unsteady hands. But Marsh managed to let them in, kick the door shut and start kissing her all at the same time.

She wrapped her arms round his neck. His long body pressed against hers. She lost all sense of time as his mouth moved against hers. She felt his runner's muscles under her fingertips when she laid her hand on his chest. His kisses grew more frantic as he pulled her towards the bedroom, leaving a trail of coats, hats, and scarves.

When it came to it, Marsh's hands were not unsteady. Not one little bit.

11

An alarm beeped and someone turned it off. Jane sank back into sleep.

Sometime later she woke up again. She wasn't in her own bed.

Barely a second later, she remembered whose bed she was in. A thrill ran through her. Eyes still shut, she savoured the morning. She heard a shower running. She was wearing one of Marsh's T-shirts, with a faded logo for a university running event. It was clearly a well-loved T-shirt. Somehow, that seemed endearing.

She hauled herself upright and looked around. The curtains were drawn, but the bedside lamp shed enough light to see pale blue walls holding a couple of framed photo-montages. A large wardrobe and chest of drawers made the room feel cramped. On the other side of the room were a wicker basket with a shirt hanging out and a plastic basket holding loosely folded clothes. A sock that had missed its mark lay between them, as though unsure which pile it belonged to.

She remembered Polly's definition of heterosexual men when she saw the line of clothes lying where they'd dropped them on their way to the bed.

The sound of the shower stopped. Jane leapt out of bed and scrabbled around to find her underwear. When she heard the bathroom door open, she jumped back into the bed and hurriedly finger-combed her hair.

Marsh came in, buttoning his shirt. 'Morning,' he said with a smile.

He looked so delicious with his hair wet and his feet still bare. Jane felt herself melt all over again.

'Hi,' she said, and knew she'd gone bright red.

He picked a pair of clean socks out of the basket on his way to the bed. 'Did you sleep OK?'

Jane thought of the night's activities. 'Well . . . '

Marsh laughed. 'I meant after that.' He leaned forward and kissed her, very gently. 'I'll go get you a cup of coffee.'

Jane wondered exactly what one said the morning after the first night. It had been much easier with Ashby. They'd just fallen into bed together and stayed there for three days. Today she'd have to go back to work.

She closed her eyes and groaned. 'Work. I'd forgotten about that. Can I use your shower?'

'Sure. There's some of Stevie's stuff in the cupboard, just use whatever you want.' He went to the door. 'I'll go put the kettle on.'

The top shelf of the bathroom cupboard was full of shaving foam and other male toiletries. The bottom shelf had a few half used bottles from The Body Shop, and, rather incongruously, a very expensive perfume. Jane lifted the lid and breathed in. Marshall's sister certainly had sophisticated taste in fragrance. Why had Stevie chosen to leave her posh perfume behind? She carefully put the bottle back and looked through the various scrubs and lotions for shower gel.

Feeling much more awake after the shower, she dressed in the only clothes she had. Fortunately her shirt wasn't too wrinkled. Once she'd pulled her hair into a ponytail, she checked her appearance in the mirror outside the bathroom. There was a glow about her and her eyes sparkled.

Marsh was tapping away at his laptop in the kitchen. 'I've made toast.'

He closed the computer and ushered her towards the breakfast bar where a pile of toast and an assortment of jams was waiting. 'I wasn't sure what you liked on your toast.' He put a mug of coffee in front of her.

'Jam's fine,' said Jane as she began to butter toast.

After several minutes of silence, Marsh ventured to speak.

'Well, this is awkward.'

Jane looked up. 'But, not in a bad way.'

'No, not in a bad way.'

They both munched their toast for a moment without making eye contact. Finally Marsh cleared his throat. 'Jane.'

She looked up.

'I . . . really like you.' He didn't quite meet her eyes. 'And I'd love to see you again . . . you know . . . outside of work.'

'But?'

'Well, there's work. Like I said before, the whole intra-office relationship thing. I've already been cautioned about it once and . . . '

Was he going to say he didn't want to see her again, now that he'd slept with her? She chided herself for thinking that the night before had been anything more than a one night stand. How could she have been so stupid?

She looked at her plate to hide the tears that threatened. 'I understand that. I don't want to get you into trouble. So, if you don't want to meet like this again . . . '

'No, no,' he said, eyes wide. 'That's not what I meant. I meant . . . can we keep things discreet at work? You know, pretend nothing's going on?'

'Of course, I can do that.' She knew her relief showed in her voice. 'For a moment there, I thought . . . Never mind.'

Marsh reached across and took her hand. 'I really, really like you.' He looked into her eyes. 'I have from the moment I ran into you in the street. And each time I get to know a bit more about you, I like you more. I wasn't going to suggest we treat last night as a one-off.' His dimple appeared. 'I don't think I could bear that.'

'That's good. I kind of enjoyed myself last night too.' She felt another blush creep up her cheeks.

Marsh brought her hand up and placed a gentle kiss on her palm.

Later, as Marsh packed up his bag, he said, 'Jane, what happened to that paper you found last night? Is it still on my desk?'

Jane thought back to the highly charged moments of the night before. 'I think Keith has it.' In her haste, she hadn't even thought to ask for it back.

Marsh grimaced.

'It's no big deal. I can always print another copy.'

'It's not that. It's Keith. I bet he takes the credit for it.'

Jane gaped. She knew he and Keith didn't get on particularly well, but she didn't think either of them would lower themselves to such a level. 'He wouldn't do that, would he? It's not exactly professional.'

Marsh gave her an unreadable look. 'I wouldn't be so sure.'

'I'm sure it'll be OK.'

Marsh said nothing and went back to cramming papers into his bag.

The walk to the train station was very different from the one the night before. They walked briskly, but without urgency. It was still quite early, but the sky was turning soft pastel pink and birds were singing. Jane felt as if she was walking on air.

As they neared the station Marsh said, 'Perhaps it would be better if we catch different trains. You catch the first one that comes. I'll catch the one after that. That way we'll arrive a few minutes apart.'

'It wouldn't do to turn up together.' She started to smile, but then remembered she was still wearing yesterday's clothes. Her smile faded.

'What's wrong?'

'I'm just wondering if it's obvious that I'm wearing the same clothes as yesterday.'

'I hadn't thought of that.' He touched her hand. 'Don't worry. I doubt anyone will notice.'

* * *

From: Sally Thomas, To: Valerie Fenwick
Did you see what Jane had on this

morning? Was that the same top she was wearing yesterday? Sally.

From: Valerie, To: Sally
I can't say I noticed her clothes, but I did think she was in a good mood this morning. I'll ask Ruth if there's any gossip. Better go. Marsh has left a whole load of tapes for me to do. I guess he was working late last night again. I hope he gets this promotion. I could do with a bit more cash. Besides, he generates so much work for me, I may as well be a partner's secretary! Val.

From: Keith Durridge, To Susan Jameson
Hi Susan. I've found a paper that discusses using the two relevant classes of drugs together. Which means, by default, it mentions the overall classes of drugs, which we can use against the patent I'm dealing with too. I am booking a meeting to discuss. Keith.

From: Eric, To: Keith
My secretary tells me that the lovely Jane is wearing the same clothes as yesterday. As I haven't had a boastful email from you, do I take it that someone else has beaten you to it? Eric.

From: Keith, To: Eric
Yes, the gossip has reached me too. I should have guessed after she ran off last night. I think a change of tactic is called for. The K-man is nothing if not resourceful. Keith.

From: Keith, To: Susan
Hi Susan. I have moved the meeting so that Jane can attend. I should mention that she was the one who actually found the paper, using a search done under my guidance. Keith.

12

From: Mike Taylor, To: Ashby
How are things going with Jane?
My research suggests that having
her around does wonders for your
popularity. People saw her as an icon
of sincerity. A girl next door who
stood by her man etc. Anything you
can do to get back in her good books
and maybe get her to come to a
launch party or two would be help-
ful. Mike.

From: Ashby, To: Mike
We split up months ago. I don't even
know where she is. Can't we just do a
charity gig or something instead?

From: Mike, To: Ashby
Doing the regular stuff is important,
but the way to the mega popularity is
to get you talked about. You don't

have to get back together with Jane, just be seen together so that the speculation can start. That way, you're guaranteed to be covered by the gossip press and the mainstream stuff will follow. You said you'd do anything for the band. Well, now's your chance. Get in touch with her. And make it convincing.

From: Ashby, To: Jane
Babes. I miss you. Come back. Pleeeeeease. The band's doing really well and stuff, but things aren't the same without you. I tried calling you, but your mum won't tell me where you are! Missing you loads. Love you. Ashby.

From: Jane, To: Ashby
Leave me alone. I'm trying to get back on track after wasting four years of my life with you. Have you sorted out the flat yet? I could really do with my share of the deposit right now. Jane.

From: Ashby, To: Jane
I haven't done anything about the flat. I keep hoping you'll come back and everything will be like it was. I guess I'm hoping all this is just a bad dream and I'll wake up to find my beautiful Janie asleep next to me. A.

From: Jane, To: Ashby
You make me sick.

From: Ashby, To: Mike
Dude, she's not going for it. I still have no idea where she is.

From: Mike, To: Ashby
There isn't much time left. Launch is next week. I think we'll go to plan B. Mike.

* * *

Jane printed out two more copies of the paper. As she walked back from the print room, she noticed one of the secretaries looking at her. She turned away, telling herself she was just being paranoid. Ever since the debacle with the tabloid photographers, she tended to think she was under scrutiny wherever she went. It had been a while since she'd split up with Ashby and the magazines had moved on to different stories. She really needed to get a grip.

She had to take a copy of the paper to Marsh. She reminded herself to act casually. Not easy to do when the thought of him made her heart skip.

She stopped at the door to his office, surprised to see Keith standing at the desk, but no Marsh.

'Hello.' Keith closed the book he had been looking at. It was Marsh's desk diary.

'I was just checking when Marsh was available,' he said. 'I was going to book a meeting for all three of us with Susan to discuss this paper you found.'

Jane was about to ask why he hadn't used the usual method of booking meetings when Marsh returned.

He ignored Jane. 'What can I do for you?'

'I was just telling Jane, I think we should arrange a meeting to talk to Susan about the paper we found.'

'Good idea,' said Marsh. 'Do you want to book it, or shall I?'

'I'll do it,' Keith smiled at Jane. 'I haven't forgotten that I promised to buy you a drink. What happened last night? I waited in the lobby, but you didn't show.'

Jane raised a weak smile. 'I . . . got delayed. I must have just missed you.'

'Drink after work tonight?'

'I can't tonight, sorry.'

'Perhaps next week then. Better get back to the grind, I suppose.' He aimed a finger at Marsh. 'I'll send you a meeting request.'

'You do that,' said Marsh, equally amiably.

'See you later Jane.' Keith left.

Both she and Marsh stared after him. 'He's up to something,' Marsh said.

'He didn't take the credit for finding

the paper, did he?'

Marsh frowned thoughtfully at the space Keith had vacated.

Jane felt a little skip of happiness. He really was lovely, and she was going to see him again.

Suddenly, Marsh snapped out of his frown and looked at Jane. For a moment, they stared into each other's eyes, and the rest of the world receded. Sharp footsteps in the hallway outside broke the mood and they both looked away.

'Um . . . was that everything, Jane?' He sat down and shuffled papers on his desk. 'Did you need anything else?'

'I just wanted to give you a copy of this.' She held out the paper.

He took it, careful not to touch her hand. 'Thank you very much,' he said, and gave her a little smile.

'You're welcome.' She left before the temptation to kiss him became unbearable.

★　★　★

Text from: Polly, To: Jane
OK, miss dirty stop out. Tell me
EVERYTHING.

Text from: Jane, To: Polly
What do you expect me to say? We
were both working late. I found an
interesting paper and took it round to
show him. Things sort of happened
from there. And he is DEFINITELY not
gay ;-)

Text from: Polly, To: Jane
That's not an explanation. I want
details.

Text from: Jane, To: Polly
You'll have to wait until I see you. I
have tons of work to do. Especially if
I want to have any time off at the
weekend.

13

CAUSE CELEB: The Magazine that connects YOU to the stars.

Cause Celeb has heard that *Trip-hoppers'* star Ashby Thornton is gearing up for the launch of their next album *Swagger*. But sources say that Ashby's heart is not really in it. Twenty-five year old Ashby is still pining for his ex-girlfriend Jane Porter.

'He feels really badly about what happened,' band member and close personal friend Lee told our *Cause Celeb* reporter. 'He let fame get to him and he let go of what was really important. He has tried to contact Jane, but can't find her anywhere. He's really hurting right now.'

CAUSE CELEB CAUSE OF THE MONTH: Can YOU find Jane Porter? Contact us on causeofthemonth@causeceleb.comm

★ ★ ★

To: Marshall, From: Stevie
Hi Marsh. I've just seen the latest *Cause Celeb*. Apparently, Ashby Thornton is wanting to get back together with Jane. I know you were going to have dinner with her next week. She might be on the rebound, so please, please be careful. Just thought I'd let you know. As you say, it's probably not a good idea to date a colleague anyway. Love Stevie.

From: Marshall, To: Stevie
Thanks for the advice, but I don't really see what that has to do with anything. Anyway, it's bit too late now ;-) Marsh.

From: Stevie, To: Marshall

You don't mean . . . ? OMG! OMG! OMG! That was quick work. Especially for you. I hope you know what you're doing. Stevie.

From: James, To: Marshall
Lou tells me you've had some progress on the Jane front. What happened to waiting until after the partners' meeting? Jim.

From: Marshall, To: James
Things took an interesting turn last night . . . I'm afraid my resolve crumbled. We've agreed that we're going to keep it out of the office. She was very understanding about it. I guess the whole unwanted publicity thing that she had with her ex means she doesn't want to draw attention to herself either. Am I to take it that you, Lou and Stevie have been talking to each other? Honestly, haven't you people got anything better to do? Marsh.

From: James, To: Louise
Lou, since you insist I go and see
how Marsh is, I have done so. He
looks . . . happy. That's the only way
I can describe it. He was humming to
himself. Humming, Louise. I haven't
heard him humming since . . . god,
not for years. Not since that girl back
in the first year . . . what was her
name? The one with the scary teeth.
I'm a bit worried he's risking upsetting
the partnership, but he says he's got
it under control, so I guess we have
to leave him to it. Please don't ask me
to go and talk to him about his feelings. I'm a bloke. We don't talk about
that sort of thing without several
pints being involved. Jim.

*   *   *

Jane wriggled her freshly painted toes.
For a moment she thought wistfully of
the stylist who used to do her hair and
make-up before any big do with Ashby.
Technically, the girl had been hired to

do the hair and faces of the band, but *Triphoppers'* manager thought that Jane was an important part of their image too.

No more.

It had been two days since her night with Marsh. He kept his distance from her at work, but when they did catch each other's eye, his small half smile was enough to melt her at the knees all over again. It was safe to say that Ashby was firmly in the past now. She put the lid on the nail varnish and settled back in her chair. Beside her, Polly's landline rang.

Polly was lounging on the sofa, working, her pen between her teeth as she tapped away on her laptop. She looked up at the sound of the phone but didn't move.

'Shall I get that?' Jane was already reaching over.

'Please.'

'Jane!' Her mother's voice came, fast and breathless, as soon as Jane answered. 'Oh thank goodness. You weren't answering your mobile and I was starting to get worried.'

'Oh, sorry Mum. I've just got a new phone and I haven't got round to sending everyone the new number yet.'

'What happened to your old phone?'

She hadn't mentioned the mugging to her mother, not wanting to worry her. 'I . . . lost it.'

'Oh that is a shame. Did it cost a lot to replace?'

'Not really.'

'Anyway, the reason I've been trying to get hold of you, apart from to see how you are of course, is that Ashby has been calling for you again.'

Jane rolled her eyes. 'What does he want?'

'Well, he wants you. He says he's really sorry about what happened and he didn't know what he was thinking and he wants you to forgive him.'

'Huh.'

'He sounded really upset, darling. And he has always been good to you apart from that one time . . . Perhaps you should talk to him, see what he has to say.'

'No way. Absolutely not.'

'Now darling, are you sure?'

'Mum, we've discussed this. I am not talking to him or forgiving him. Ever. OK? If he calls again, tell him to take a running jump.'

There was a guilty silence at the other end of the line.

'Mum? What have you done?'

'Well, I did give him your mobile number.'

'My old number?'

'Yes.'

'That's dead now, thank goodness. Don't tell him anything more. OK?'

'But — '

'Mum, promise me.'

Her mother sighed. 'OK. I promise. But if you change your mind . . . '

'I know how to get hold of him, if I need to.'

Her mother sighed again. Jane changed the subject. They chatted about things not relating to Ashby for a few minutes.

When Jane hung up, Polly said, 'What was that all about?'

'Ashby's been badgering Mum for my phone number. To apologise apparently.'

Polly raised one eyebrow. 'Really? I hope she didn't give him your number.'

'Only my old one. She thinks I should contact him. You know what she's like. She thinks the sun shines out of his arse.'

'Your mum just wants to be able to invite the Beckhams to your wedding.' Her smile faded. 'It is a bit weird though, isn't it? Ashby coming over all remorseful. It doesn't sound like him.' She typed something into her laptop.

'What're you doing?'

'Just checking something out . . . ' Whatever she'd read had her frowning. 'Oh dear.'

'What?'

'We-ll . . . You know *Cause Celeb* has a cause of the month. You remember

180

how they did that 'what should Kate Winslet buy her husband for Christmas' one? And the 'can you help Chantelle find the perfect shoes for this outfit' one?'

Jane wondered where this was going as a horrible thought began to coalesce in her mind.

Polly turned the laptop around, showing her the *Cause Celeb* blog. Jane read quickly. About halfway through, she started to swear.

'I'm going to kill him. I really am going to kill him.'

★ ★ ★

From: Jane, To: Ashby
Ashby. What the hell is going on? You are supposed to be leaving me alone, remember? And now suddenly I'm the *Cause Celeb* cause of the month!! Or, more to the point, I guess, you are. Just in time for the new album launch. What a coincidence. Look, I meant what I said. I

181

haven't done you or your career any damage. In fact, I helped you as much as I could. Why can't you have the common courtesy to do the same for me? I was just getting on with my life. I have a job I like and I'm making new friends. Now, thanks to you, I have to watch my step everywhere I go, in case there's a photographer trying to get a shot of me. Again. Haven't you done enough to me already? Jane.

From: Ashby, To: Jane
Babes. The *Cause Celeb* stuff isn't really anything to do with me. We hired this new PR guy, he said it was good for the new album, so I just went along with it. Besides, it's true. I do miss you. You were a stabilising influence on me. And we had some good times, didn't we? Ashby.

From: Jane, To: Ashby
I don't care whose idea it was. Call it off. Can't you get one of your little

tarts to pretend they're going out with you? You can both get the exposure you need and you'll both be happy. What about that creature from *Hollyoaks* that you so famously cheated on me with? Seriously, if this doesn't stop and soon, I am going to see a lawyer about suing the pants off you and Mike for invasion of privacy. Jane.

From: Ashby, To: Jane
Janelle? No way. She hires brain cells by the hour. Aw come on Jane, don't be like that. Everyone will have forgotten all about you in a few weeks. Where's the harm?

From: Jane, To: Ashby
WHERE'S THE HARM??? I can't believe you. Have you not paid attention to a word I've just said? I want my life back you selfish bastard. You'll be hearing from my lawyer. Jane.

From: Jane, To: Polly
I just threatened to sue Ashby. I'm

not even sure I have a case. It's not libellous to say he misses me. Besides, I can't afford a lawyer. Help! Jane.

From: Polly, To: Jane
Jane. Relax. It's just a stupid magazine. No one's going to bother you. They'll forget about you soon enough. It'll be fine. HUGS. Pol.

From: Jane, To: Polly
I can't just forget about it, Pol. You don't know how awful it was. Every time I went out of the flat, some guy with a camera would take photos of me. I couldn't even open the curtains without someone trying to get a telephoto lens on me. I had to live in perpetual twilight for days. Even when I escaped to Mum's house, they hunted me down — although, Mum might have let that one slip. Not sure. People kept wanting me to comment on how I was feeling and what I thought of

that woman from *Hollyoaks*. All I
wanted was to be left alone. I can't
go through that again. Jane.

From: Polly, To: Jane
Try not to think about it, hon. It'll all
be OK. Honest. Just concentrate on
that nice new man of yours. Love Pol.

From: Ashby, To: Mike
Dude, Jane says to call off the press
or she'll sue. Ashby.

From: Mike, To: Ashby
Let her sue! That's publicity money
can't buy! I've arranged a photoshoot
for Tuesday 2 p.m. Tell the lads. Mike.

14

From: Sally, To: Ruth
Hi Ruth. Have you seen *Cause Celeb*
is trying to find a Jane Porter that
used to go out with Ashby Thornton.
Do you think she's the same Jane
Porter as our Jane? I've just been looking at pictures on the web. They look
vaguely similar, but it's hard to tell.
Celeb Jane is blonde and all air
brushed. Our Jane is normal looking.

From: Ruth, To: Sally
I see what you mean. There is a
resemblance. It is a bit of a coincidence, isn't it, with the same name
and Jane being from Manchester. I
noticed she doesn't talk about her
love life, which would make sense if
she was trying to get away from it.
On the other hand, she's training to
be a patent agent — it's hardly a

glam job, is it? And Porter isn't that unusual a name — maybe there are a lot of Porters in Manchester. Besides, Jane's so quiet. She wouldn't say boo to a goose. I don't know. I'm inclined to think it's just a massive coincidence. But I'll keep an eye out for other clues. Ruth.

* * *

Jane was so flustered by being the focus of *Cause Celeb* that she couldn't concentrate. It was nearly lunchtime, so she grabbed her coat and left, telling Ruth she was going to get a sandwich. There were several sandwich shops nearby, most of which had people queuing. Recalling seeing a soup place not too far away, she walked in that direction. When someone called her name, she turned and saw Keith, running to catch up with her.

'Going out for lunch?' He was wearing a long black coat and what looked like a university scarf.

Jane considered lying and saying she was going to the bank, but she had a feeling that no matter what she said, he was going to try to join her. She didn't reply.

'I'll come with you,' said Keith, as if she'd welcomed his approach. He fell in beside her.

Jane was reminded of leaving the office with Marsh a couple of nights before. How different an experience that had been.

'I know a nice place that does a lovely plate of couscous,' Keith said, as they turned a corner.

She didn't want to have lunch with Keith. On the other hand, if she got a soup and took it back to the office, she would have to sit in the canteen and listen to the gossip, which she really didn't feel like doing.

'It'll be fun. A nice hot lunch.' He looked at her, his expression faintly pleading. It suddenly occurred to her that, for all his bravado, he might be quite insecure. Perhaps his constant invitations to the pub stemmed partially from the fact that he was lonely.

'I won't take no for an answer,' he said.

Deciding she had nothing to lose by getting to know him a bit better, Jane went with him.

They passed the row of high street shops and bagel bars where she normally bought lunch. Keith ushered her past an impressive looking, pink stone building and down a lane. It opened into a crowded street market. There were stalls selling cheap jumpers. A man in a tracksuit shouted his wares, his breath condensing in the cold air. Men and women in suits rummaged through stalls selling imitation designer goods. Stallholders stood around chatting.

'Leather Lane market,' Keith said. He led her past various stalls, and finally guided her through a gap between a man selling jewellery and a dreadlocked woman who was selling dried fruit.

The front of the Moroccan café bore brightly coloured sheets of paper announcing meals for a few pounds. When the door opened to let a group of women out, Jane and Keith squeezed inside.

The shop was beautifully warm and the air was heavy with the smell of cinnamon and cumin. On one side was a counter with steaming tureens of stew. Opposite, plastic tables were crammed together, with people huddled around them, laughing and chatting as they tucked into plates heaped with couscous and sauce. The place was filled with voices and the clatter of cutlery.

Keith leaned close to speak in her ear. 'What would you like?'

Jane pointed at an appetising looking vegetable stew.

'I'll get it,' said Keith. 'You find us a table. There's more room at the back.'

She headed in the direction he pointed. The back room was small and equally crowded. As she hovered by the doorway, a couple finished their meal and stood up. She immediately grabbed their vacated table.

As she waited she stacked up the used plates and wiped the table. Doing so reminded her of having been a waitress in her student days. Looking round, she felt a wave of nostalgia. This was the sort of place she and Ashby would have gone to for lunch as a treat. He had been fun and interesting, not the self-absorbed pop brat he now was.

Jane imagined Marshall here with her. She could see similarities between him and the Ashby she'd fallen for all those years ago. It was an unsettling thought.

A waiter whisked the stack of plates away. He wiped the table down with a wet cloth, leaving a slippery smear behind. 'Enjoy your meal,' he said.

Jane folded her hands on her lap, not touching the tabletop. She knew she shouldn't compare Marsh to Ashby, but she couldn't help it. She thought about her time with Marsh a few nights before. In some ways, Marsh and Ashby were very different indeed.

She was still smiling when Keith arrived with two heaped plates. She reached for her purse to pay for hers, but he dismissed it with a wave. 'I know you've got cashflow problems until your new cards come through. So, tuck in. It's on me.'

'Thanks.' Just as she raised the first forkful to her mouth, her phone rang. Marsh's name came up on the display. Mouthing 'Excuse me' to Keith, she answered it.

'Hi, it's me. Marsh.' He paused, as though unsure what to say. 'Um . . . are you in the office at the moment?'

'No.'

'Great. Listen, I was wondering . . . '

'Yes . . . ' Jane prompted.

'Would you like to come over to my place for the weekend? We could loaf around town a bit and . . . do stuff.'

Keith was making a great show of pretending he wasn't listening. She wondered how much of what Marsh was saying was audible to Keith. 'That sounds good.'

There was a short silence from the other end. 'Is there someone else there?'

'Oh yes.' She felt oddly guilty that she was out with another man, and reminded herself that she and Marshall weren't really an item yet. And she was only having lunch with a colleague. It wasn't like a date. She knew Marshall and Keith didn't see eye to eye, but that was no reason for her not to interact with Keith. After all, Marshall's dislike could be misplaced.

'OK. I'd best let you go then,' Marshall said. 'I'll call you after work this evening and we'll sort out a time to meet. See you later.'

'Yes. Thanks for calling,' she said, trying to sound casual for Keith's benefit. 'Bye.'

'That was the estate agent,' she said as she put her phone away. She hoped it sounded convincing. 'I'm looking for a place to stay.'

'Really? I thought you were staying with a friend.'

'I am, sort of. It's her spare room; she normally uses it as a study, so it's really tiny. There's barely room to walk around the bed. It's a bit like being a student again.' She picked up her fork and started to eat. The food was surprisingly good. 'This is lovely.'

'Isn't it?' said Keith. 'I come here a lot. Although, it's much more fun in company. I usually end up getting a takeaway and having it back at work.'

Again Jane wondered if he was lonely.

'I bet you don't get this sort of diversity up in Yorkshire,' he said.

'Lancashire,' she corrected. 'I'm from Manchester. That's in Lancashire.'

Keith shrugged. 'Sorry, I've never really got to grips with the difference. I'm a London boy, you see. The rest of the country is just 'not London' to me.' He grinned, as if to take the sting out of his words.

As the meal went on, they talked about work and life. For some reason Keith had stopped trying to make a pass at her. Without the threat of lechery, Jane found he was surprisingly good company. When it was time to go back, she was genuinely sorry.

'You know Jane,' said Keith, as they walked back to the office, 'I think we got off on the wrong foot. I know I can come across as a little . . . brash. It's like a nervous tick I have when I meet new people. I open my mouth and this horrendous crap comes out. It takes me a while to relax and be myself, if you see what I mean.'

She had suspected as much and felt sorry for judging him too hastily. She was glad she hadn't let herself be influenced by Marshall's prejudices and had taken the time to talk to Keith. 'That's OK. I wasn't offended by your anti-Northern stance.'

'Oh that was for real,' he said, grinning. 'Can't stand Yorkshiremen.'

Jane laughed too. 'Nowt good never came out of Yorkshire,' she said solemnly. ''Cept road to Lancashire.'

Keith roared with laughter. 'Is that a real saying?'

'Oh yes. We Lancashire folk don't get on with Yorkshire folk. Well known fact.'

'What, county rivalry? Like Kent and Essex?'

'If you like.'

'Brilliant. I shall have to remember that,' Keith said, as they arrived at the entrance to their building. 'Now, alas, I have to love you and leave you. I've got to get this opinion written by tomorrow and I haven't read half the documents yet.' He held the door open for her. 'It was nice talking to you properly. We should do this again sometime.'

Jane nodded. 'That would be nice,' she said. And meant it.

15

From: Stevie, To: Marshall
Guess what Marsh, Buzz and I are
coming down to London tonight to
go to a gig. We'll be crashing at the
flat after. Hope that's OK with you.
We're probably not going out until
about ten, so fancy grabbing some
takeout with us? Love Stevie.

From: Marshall, To: Stevie
I'm supposed to be inviting Jane over
. . . I'll postpone if you guys are going
to be there. I don't want to miss the
opportunity to meet the famous Buzz.
Will you two be staying the whole
weekend? Marsh.

From: Stevie, To: Marshall
Shit. I forgot about Jane. Look, we'll
find somewhere else to stay. Don't
worry about it.

From: Marshall, To: Stevie
No, that's fine. It will be nice to see you and to meet Buzz. I can always have Jane round on Saturday. So long as you're not planning to stay the whole weekend . . . ?

From: Stevie, To: Marshall
We'll clear off on Saturday after-noon, I promise. Can I meet Jane? It's only fair if you get to meet my boyfriend.

From: Marshall, To: Stevie
No. You can't meet her. Sorry. I've only seen her twice outside of work. I'd like to get to know her better before I introduce her to my sister.

From: Stevie, To: Marshall
From what I've heard you know her pretty well after yesterday. But fear not, brother dear. We'll be out of your hair by Saturday afternoon. Gotta go. Train in twenty minutes. See you later. Love Stevie.

From: Marshall, To: James
Drat. I was planning to cook a nice meal for Jane and Stevie emails to say that she and her no good boyfriend are coming down for the weekend. Much as I love Stevie, she somehow manages to throw a spanner in my romantic aspirations. On the other hand, I get to meet Buzz, finally. I'll be interested to see if he is as in love with her as she is with him. Marsh.

From: James, To: Marshall
You shouldn't prejudge the poor guy, you know. Sounds like Stevie really likes him, so it is possible he's totally besotted with her too. He may genuinely mean to pay back everything he's borrowed from her. Just because you were ultra sensible with money when you were a student, it doesn't mean everyone has to be. Jim.

From: James, To: Marshall
PS: Are you going to let Stevie have this Buzz guy sleeping in her room

and risk them having sex while you're in the building? Or are you going to make him sleep on the sofa? Jim.

From: Marshall, To: James
Ugh. Why did you just do that? I hadn't even thought about it and now you've put it in my head. I'm guessing I don't have any choice in the matter anyway, she's too old for me to dictate that sort of thing now. Just you wait until Molly's old enough to have a boyfriend. I'm going to remind you of this. Marsh.

★ ★ ★

Work was becoming increasingly difficult. Despite the demanding deadlines on each new case, Jane was having trouble keeping her mind on the job. Her thoughts kept straying towards Marsh, who was only a flimsy office wall away from her. Occasionally, she would catch herself staring at the plasterboard, daydreaming to the muffled sound of his voice.

So far, she had managed to avoid bumping into him too often, but all her senses had been on high alert all day. As a result she felt physically and emotionally exhausted. It was almost a relief to be away from the office and back at the flat. She dug her keys out of her new bag and, remembering the last time, knocked. Loudly.

Polly pulled the door open. 'You don't have to keep hammering on the door like that. It won't happen again.'

'Better safe than sorry,' said Jane, laughing.

'Do you want a glass of wine? I was thinking wine and DVDs tonight.' She gestured to the bottle on the coffee table.

'I'm sorry, Pol. I've got plans.' Giving Polly an apologetic smile, Jane hung up her handbag and coat and headed towards her room.

'Where's he taking you tonight?' Polly shouted after her.

'He's going to call me to sort out a time and place.' She returned to the living room and fished her new phone out of her bag. Looking meaningfully at Polly, she took it into the bathroom with her.

★   ★   ★

Refreshed after her shower, Jane spent a few minutes in her room, blow-drying her hair so that it fell smoothly around her face. She was sitting on the bed, using a mirror that was propped on a bookcase to apply her make-up when Polly knocked.

'It's open,' she said.

Polly put her head round the door. 'I've poured you a glass of wine.' Her eyes drifted to the phone, which was lying on the bed, next to Jane. 'Did he ring?'

'Not yet,' Jane looked at her watch. Seven o'clock. Perhaps Marsh was still at work.

'He's probably on his way home.

There's no reception on the underground.'

Jane set her eyeliner pencil aside and
stood. 'I think I'll come have that glass
of wine in the living room.'

She followed Polly out and flopped
onto the sofa. 'Where's Andy tonight?'
She picked up the glass of wine Polly
had poured.

'Never mind him,' said Polly. 'Let's
talk about your fella. I need a fix of
vicarious excitement. It's just so . . .
romantic. I haven't had excitement like
that in . . . oh, years.'

'But you've got Andy. And you love
each other. All I've had so far is one
night.' Her gaze slid to the phone. Until
now, she had been confident there was
more to it than that, but the fact that
Marsh hadn't rung yet was starting to
worry her.

'He'll call.' As if on cue, the phone
rang. Polly gave a little squeak.

Jane picked up the phone and walked
towards the kitchen.

'Hi Jane, it's Marsh.'

There was an awkward silence. Jane felt a creeping sense of unease. 'Marsh?'

'Jane, I'm really sorry, but I'm going to have to postpone meeting up. My sister and her boyfriend are descending on the flat tonight . . . '

'OK,' said Jane, her mood starting to sink. 'Do you want to go out instead?'

'Well, I'd love to, but I really want to meet this guy . . . the boyfriend, I mean. I think he's . . . well, he's my sister's boyfriend. I should meet him.' He sighed. 'Jane, I'm really sorry to mess you about like this. Would you mind if we met up tomorrow instead? Stevie assures me they'll clear off by lunchtime, so we'd have the flat to ourselves for the rest of the weekend.'

'Um . . . ' Jane stared at the shelves in the kitchen. He didn't want to see her that night. Perhaps he was having second thoughts. What should she say now? She didn't want to sound like she didn't care, but at the same time she didn't want to seem needy. She thought of the night they'd spent together and tears started to threaten. She blinked them back.

'Jane?' Marsh sounded anxious. 'Are you still there?'

Jane cleared her throat. 'Uh-huh.'

'Jane, I promise you, I'm not playing mind games with you. I really truly do want to see you, but Stevie just dropped this on me with no notice.'

'Right.'

'So, tomorrow . . . ?'

Jane turned around. Polly was sitting on the sofa, watching. If she said no to Marsh, she would have to put up with Polly's questions all weekend. 'Sure,' she said, almost a sigh. 'Why not.'

'Brilliant! Shall I meet you in Covent Garden? At about eleven?'

'OK,' said Jane. She listened while he described the place to meet.

'Sounds good,' she said, trying not to let disappointment into her voice. 'I'll see you tomorrow.'

'Yes. I'm looking forward to it.'

'Me too.' Her voice came out too soft. 'I'd better go. Bye.'

'Bye.'

She hung up and stood still, staring at the phone, not sure how she felt.

'Jane?' Polly came up behind her. 'What was that all about?'

'He postponed until tomorrow lunchtime. His sister's introducing him to her boyfriend or something.'

'And?'

Jane sighed. 'And nothing, I guess. I'd just mentally prepared myself for seeing him tonight, that's all.'

Polly took her arm and propelled her towards the sofa. She thrust the glass of wine into Jane's hand. 'That's not it, is it?' She sat beside Jane and picked up her own glass.

Jane took a sip of wine. She closed her eyes and savoured the warmth of the alcohol going down her throat. Why was she so upset? It was just a cancelled date, with a perfectly plausible explanation. But then Ashby had always had plausible explanations for his sudden absences. A jam session with the guys, a meeting with their manager, going out for a drink after a recording. All very good reasons for his not coming home when he should. But only half of them had been true.

'This is about Ashby, isn't it?'

Jane opened her eyes. 'What?'

'Just because Ashby lied to you doesn't mean that everyone else is going to lie to you too.'

'I know that.'

'So, why is the fact that Marsh postponed your date bothering you so much? It's not like he cancelled on you.'

'I don't know. I just can't shake this feeling that something's not right.'

Polly leaned forward and took Jane's hand. 'Jane, we've been friends since we were ten. I know you. Before this stuff with Ashby, you wouldn't have had a problem with someone moving a date. You were such a trusting person.'

'Yes, and look where that got me. Not only did he cheat on me, he publicly humiliated me. I don't know which is worse.'

'Honey, I know he hurt you, but you really do have to let it go.'

'How can I? I loved Ashby. I thought he loved me too. Then I find out that for months I'd been living a lie. How can I just forget that and move on like it never happened? I let it happen once, how do I know it's not going to happen again? Maybe I've got 'use me, I'm a sap' written on my forehead. Maybe I'm just a terrible judge of character.' Tears welled and she squashed them away with her palm.

Polly squeezed her arm. 'You're a nice person, Jane. It doesn't mean you're a sap. When you first met Ashby, he was basically a nice person too. You guys were well suited. It's just that when he suddenly became famous, it went to his head a bit. He changed. It's not your fault.'

'But how did I not see it coming?'

'Who would? You were happy for him and as supportive as it was humanly possible to be. There's no way you could have known that he was going to be seduced by a tart from *Hollyoaks*.'

Jane stared into her drink. A tear rolled down her cheek. 'She wasn't the only one,' she said, her voice barely above a whisper. 'There were others. One night stands, mostly. Pete from the band told me. He felt bad for covering for Ash. Everyone knew, Pol. Everyone but me.'

'Oh Jane.' Polly scooted close and hugged her. 'Oh Jane, I'm so sorry.'

Jane buried her face in Polly's shoulder. 'I feel so . . . used.' She had kept this extra news to herself for months, not wanting to add to the evidence of just how gullible she had been. Now that she had told Polly, she felt an odd sense of release. Tears flowed, but she did nothing to stop them. Polly held her, as always, a source of comfort.

'You can't let him poison everything else for you too,' said Polly, after some time. 'You've met someone new now. You like this Marsh guy, right?'

Jane nodded.

'Well, you have to give him a chance then. You can't let Ashby ruin this for you.'

Jane leaned back and stared at Polly's earnest face.

'From what I can tell,' said Polly, 'all Marsh's done is postpone a date. That's hardly a crime. Did he say he really wanted to see you?'

Jane nodded.

'And you still want to see him?'

'Yes.'

'Well then.' Polly spread her hands. 'Why don't you give it a chance?'

Polly was right. She thought of Marsh's shy smile. Could she really compare that to Ashby's confident grin? Everything she knew about Marsh made him the polar opposite of Ashby. He was analytical, where Ashby was creative; he was caring, where Ashby was self-centred; and he was a thoughtful lover where Ashby had relied on youthful enthusiasm. Surely, it wasn't so hard to believe that he would be honest where Ashby was not.

She wiped the tears off her face. 'You're right. I'm just being silly.'

Polly gave her a fond smile. 'That's my girl.' She returned to her own chair. Picking up the bottle of wine, she topped up both glasses. She raised hers. 'Besides, you're not such a bad judge of character. You picked me for a best friend.'

Jane smiled back and clinked her glass against Polly's.

'Since neither of us has any plans tonight,' said Polly. 'How about we get a DVD and some chocolate and have a girly night in?'

★ ★ ★

Jane woke up the next morning feeling strangely light-headed. So much so, she wondered if she was still drunk from the night before. Rather than making things worse, sharing her sorrow about Ashby's betrayal had somehow loosened the grip he had on her. She wished she had told Polly sooner. She hummed to herself as she brushed her teeth.

Back in her room, she pulled out her suitcase and surveyed her clothes. She needed something that was casual, but sexy. It was inconvenient, having only her work clothes and a few pairs of jeans at Polly's. She could hardly wait to move into her own place, so she could bring the rest of her clothes down from her mum's attic.

She made a mental note to contact Ashby again and try to get the deposit cheque from him. And then it occurred to her that she had just thought about Ashby without the familiar ache stirring in her stomach. Perhaps it was a good thing she had spent the previous evening with Polly and not Marsh.

After trying on several outfits, she settled on jeans, T-shirt and a cowl necked jumper that hugged her slim figure, whilst making her breasts look larger than they were. She packed a spare top and some underwear into a small bag and went into the kitchen, still humming. She was halfway through her breakfast when Polly shuffled in, wearing her dressing gown.

'Morning,' said Jane.

Polly waved in her direction and poured herself a cup of coffee. 'You look nice. And cheerful.' She popped some bread into the toaster. 'Looking forward to the rest of weekend?' she said, with a wicked grin.

Jane grinned back. 'Yes, you could say that.'

'I'm almost jealous,' Polly said. 'What have I got to look forward to? A trip to the cinema, if I'm lucky. He's not a great romantic, my Andy.'

'Oh, stop moaning. You'll have the flat to yourselves for the weekend. And don't pretend you'll spend it watching DVDs.'

Polly laughed. 'I'm glad you're in a better mood.'

'Thank you. I think I really needed to get things out of my system.'

'I'm glad you did,' said Polly. 'Any time you need to talk to someone, I'm here for you. You know that.'

'I know.' She gave Polly a quick hug. 'And I really appreciate it.'

'It was nothing.' Polly gave her a little push. 'Now get going. You're making me feel all frumpy with your long legs and nice jumper. Shoo.'

16

Text from: Stevie, To: Marshall
We r leaving at 2 & the flat is all urs.
I'd like 2 say it was nice, but it wasn't
rly. Did u have 2 be so rude 2 Buzz?
What's got into u?

Text from: Marshall, To: Stevie
I wasn't rude. I just told him to mind
his own business. I didn't want to
discuss the possible value of the flat
with him. Nor talk about how your
trust fund works. Please try and leave
the flat in a reasonable state. Like
clear up after you have breakfast. The
kitchen was a disaster this morning.
What did you do when you got in? It
sounded pretty raucous around two in
the morning. I'm surprised Mrs Watkins didn't come storming round.

Text from: Stevie, To: Marshall

Will u listen to urself? Any I would think u were in your 50s. Lighten up! Just cos I needed looking after when I was a kid doesn't mean u need to now. I'm over 18 and I can do what I like. Can't believe Mum & Dad gave u power over my money until I'm 21. Bet they didn't realise you'd be such a despot about it. Don't worry, we'll leave the flat in a good state so u can show ur precious gf round.

Text from: Marshall, To: Stevie
Look, I'm just worried about you. I know you think you love this guy, but believe me, he doesn't love you. You're just too close to see it. He'll keep borrowing money from you until you refuse and then he'll leave.

Text from: Stevie, To: Marshall
Oh yeah, cos ur such an expert on relationships. I word: DOMINIQUE. I don't have to listen to u any more. I'm an adult now.

Text from: Marshall, To: Stevie
Perhaps you should start acting like
one, then.

Text from: Stevie, To: Marshall
Fuck off.

From: Marshall, To: James
Well, I finally met the famous Buzz.
And, I hate to say it, but I think I was
right. From the moment he got there,
he was looking round with a calculating eye. I don't trust him.
Unfortunately, Stevie seems to be
totally besotted by him. I'm not sure
what she sees in him. He doesn't
even appear to be very clean. Marsh.

⋆   ⋆   ⋆

Jane looked round the crowded coffee
shop and didn't see Marsh. Doubt
wriggled into her mind. Had he stood
her up?

Maybe she had been too optimistic
about him. Perhaps it was a blessing in

disguise. She wasn't even sure she wanted another relationship so soon after Ashby.

As she turned to leave, she spotted Marsh, at a back table frowning at his BlackBerry, with a cup of coffee and a half eaten muffin on the table. He appeared to be concentrating on what he was doing. He hadn't stood her up. He was waiting for her, just as he'd said he would be.

Jane remembered her conversation with Polly the night before. She couldn't let Ashby ruin her chances of finding someone new. She lifted her chin and started towards him.

Because she was looking directly at him, she saw the exact moment he noticed her. His face lit up and he smiled, like a child on Christmas morning. His whole body seemed to become lighter as he scrambled to his feet. The doubts in Jane's mind evaporated, replaced by a thrill of pleasure. No one had looked that delighted to see her in years.

Weaving her way among the tables felt almost as if she was taking a journey from the office to a different world. When she said 'Hi,' she felt as if they were meeting after a long separation.

He leaned forward and kissed her lightly on the lips. 'You look . . . fabulous.'

Jane giggled. She was used to the phrase, having heard it shrieked between air kisses many times when she'd been with Ashby, but she had never heard any sincerity behind it.

This time it sounded heartfelt. At that moment, she felt fabulous.

'Do you want a coffee?' He slipped his BlackBerry into his jacket pocket.

She shook her head. 'What's the plan for today?'

'What would you like to do? I'm all yours.' He paused. 'In a manner of speaking.'

Jane had to laugh. 'I'd quite like to see London. You know, do touristy stuff. I've been here a few months now, but I haven't really done the sightseeing thing yet.' She didn't mention the reason was that she still hadn't got over the fear of photographers jumping out at her.

'Touristy stuff it is, then.' Casually he gestured, offering to take her overnight bag.

Astounded, she let him take the small girly bag and sling it over his shoulder. Ashby would not have been seen dead carrying a bag with daisies embroidered on it. Marsh didn't seem to care. He took her hand and together they walked out into the overcast London day.

★   ★   ★

It took Jane a while to relax. She was still half expecting people to stare and point. At first, she kept reminding herself that the man holding her hand wasn't a pop star, but a normal, non-glamorous patent lawyer, and that in London no one knew or cared who she was. Once she finally loosened up, helped considerably by a nice lunch and a glass of wine, she felt a warm sense of happiness as she and Marsh walked along the packed streets.

In the evening, they stopped to watch the sun set over the Thames. As it disappeared, the meagre heat of the day went with it. Jane shivered.

Marsh, who had his arm round her, shrugged off his jacket and draped it on her shoulders. Standing behind her, he wrapped his arms around her waist and pulled her gently to him. The coat was comfortingly warm and smelled faintly of him. She leaned back against his broad chest and sighed. How could she have even thought of not coming out with him? How long had it been since she had felt so cherished?

She turned her head and looked up.

'It's getting cold,' he said with a smile. 'Shall we go home?'

Her heart responded by increasing its pace. 'Let's.'

He continued to gaze at her for a

moment before lowering his head to kiss her.

In that brief moment Jane felt like she was the most beautiful woman in the world.

★   ★   ★

Jane sank into the sofa in Marsh's flat and stretched her legs out. The day's walking had tired her out. Marsh was pouring wine. Her senses were so attuned to him that she was aware of where he was, even when she couldn't see him.

'Here you go,' Marsh handed her a wine glass. Moving the remote control, he sat down next to her, leaned back and put his arm round her.

His body felt deliciously warm and solid. She took a sip of wine, enjoying the moment. They were still getting to know each other and real life hadn't stepped in to spoil it all. She savoured the feeling of his arm around her and the gentle tug in her stomach that told her she fancied him.

Marsh placed a kiss on the top of her head, which made things just that bit closer to perfect. 'What do you want to do tomorrow?' He flicked on the telly. There was a chat show on.

'Don't mind,' Jane murmured and half closed her eyes.

'I'll just check the weather. We could have a picnic in Hyde Park, if it's sunny.' He moved slightly to pull out his phone.

'That sounds lovely.'

'We might be in luck.'

On the TV, the show cut to the live band. A familiar voice sounded in song. Jane's eyes flew open. She sat up and reached for the remote control.

'Isn't that your ex?'

Jane stared at him. He knew? How long had he known? Who else knew?

Marsh returned her stare. 'What's the matter?'

'I — ' She tucked a strand of hair behind her ear. 'I didn't think anyone knew, that's all.'

Marsh looked embarrassed. 'Stevie told me.'

She had been so been so convinced that she could keep her past secret, but she had been wrong. What else was she wrong about? And who else knew?

'Jane?' said Marsh. 'Are you OK?'

To her surprise, she felt tears prickle. She blinked them back.

He turned the TV off. After a long, mutual silence Marsh said, 'It must have been exciting, being a pop star's girlfriend.'

There was something in his voice that made her look up. It suddenly occurred to her that he might be worried about how he would compare to Ashby. Even though Marsh seemed confident enough, wouldn't he wonder about the glamorous world she used to inhabit?

She was about to assure him that she didn't draw comparisons when she realised that she had been doing just that all day. Admittedly, Marsh had come out better in contrast to Ashby, but that didn't alter the fact that Ashby had been in the back of her mind. Perhaps it was better to be honest. Marsh was a nice man and didn't deserve to feel like he was playing second fiddle to her famous ex. 'It was OK. But it got a bit boring after a while.'

'Boring?' He raised an eyebrow. 'Hanging out with the rich and famous and going to parties doesn't sound all that boring.'

'It was, really. I mean, that life can be fun to start with, but then it becomes a bit samey. You obsess over everything — the dress, the shoes, the jewellery, the lip gloss. How's it going to look? Is it fashionable enough? Is it too fashionable? When you get somewhere, everyone gives everyone the once over. You never know who's going to try to stab you in the back in the next day's paper.

'Everyone's nerves are so stretched that they practically twang when they walk. The only way you get through it is to have a drink. So you have a glass of champagne, you try and chat to people and not make a fool of yourself. When it gets so late that you don't think you'll make it into work the next day, you call a taxi and go home. And then you get about two hours sleep and drag yourself into work. It's horrible.

'I only went because Ashby wanted me to. I didn't enjoy it much. I felt pretty inferior most of the time, to be honest.'

Marsh was watching her intently. His expression was unreadable. 'Inferior?'

Jane grimaced. 'Everyone at those parties is either glamorous or talented or rich. Sometimes all three. Ashby used to sometimes wander off to talk to 'useful contacts'.' She made air quotes with her hands. 'And I'd end up talking to a businessman in a suit who was worth a fortune.'

It suddenly occurred to her that some of Ashby's 'useful contacts' may have been other women. What had he really got up to when he'd disappeared for long stretches of time?

The minute the thought occurred to her, she knew the answer. How could she have been so stupid?

Marsh was still watching her. 'Sounds to me,' he said, slowly, 'like this Ashby guy is an idiot.'

Jane couldn't help smiling. 'That's your considered opinion, is it?'

'Trust me. I'm a lawyer.'

Jane had to laugh.

When Marsh kissed her, she leaned into him and kissed him back, trying not to spill her wine. With her free hand, she reached up to touch his hair. He drew her closer. Just as she was about to abandon herself to his kiss completely, her stomach rumbled. Embarrassed, she wriggled loose. 'Sorry.'

When he simply looked into her eyes for a moment, she thought he was going to kiss her again. Instead, he smiled. 'You're right. We'd better get something to eat.'

He leaned closer, until his lips were millimetres away from hers. 'You can't do interesting things on an empty stomach.' He placed the lightest of kisses on her lips and stood, leaving Jane to chide her stomach for ruining the moment.

★   ★   ★

Sunday evening, when Marsh offered to see Jane home, she hesitated. Much as she enjoyed herself with him, she didn't really want him to come to Polly's flat. Her relationship with him was too new and she didn't want Polly to meet him yet. She liked the fact that no one knew about them. She wanted to keep this relationship her precious private secret for as long as she could.

When she didn't reply immediately, Marsh shrugged. 'If you'd rather I didn't, that's OK too.'

'It's not that I don't want you to see me home. It's just that it's Polly's flat and it'd be a bit awkward. I'm really sorry.'

'I understand. Really.' He kissed her.

'I guess. I'll see you at work.'

'That's going to be weird.'

'Yes. Very. It's so hard to be near you and not be able to do this.' He pulled her towards him with his hands at her waist and kissed her just below her ear. Slowly he worked his way down to her collarbone, kissing all the way.

Jane melted. How was she ever going to be able to think about anything at work tomorrow? She wriggled in his grasp. 'Stop it,' she said, half-heartedly. 'That's too nice.'

Marsh pulled away, grinning. 'You're sure?'

Jane sighed and laid her head against him. 'Yes. It's getting late. I should go.'

He wrapped his arms around her and hugged. 'See you tomorrow then. I shall do my best to pretend I haven't seen you since Friday.'

★　★　★

From: Valerie, To: Sally, Indra
I think there's something going on

between Marsh and Jane. I just went into his office and you could feel the pheromones crackling. Not that they were doing anything, I hasten to add. It was just the way they were so jumpy. Val.

From: Sally, To: Valerie
Well, it would be about time Marsh found someone, wouldn't it? Jane seems nice enough. Certainly better suited to Marsh than Dominique. I imagine Marsh would be a bit quiet after the Northern boys she must be used to.

From: Valerie, To: Sally
Maybe she had her bit of rough and fancies going for the quiet, reliable type for a change. You don't get much more reliable than Marsh. I think he likes her. I tried to quiz him about Jane, but he changed the subject really fast and the tips of his ears went red, you know, like they do when he's embarrassed. On the other

hand, he's worried about his little sister. Do you remember little Stevie? She worked in the post room a couple of years back before she went to uni. Apparently, Marsh doesn't like her new boyfriend. Poor boy. Having to look after his sister has really messed with his perspective. It can't have been easy working, studying for his exams and looking after a teenager. You've got to admire him for managing to pass his exams!

From: Sally, To: Valerie
Oh, I admire him for a lot more than that, especially when he's in his little running shorts. Why do you think I come in so early?

From: Valerie, To: Sally
Stop it. He's young enough to be your son. You have furniture older than him.

From: Indra, To: Valerie
I overheard Eric talking to Keith and

I'm worried that they're up to their old tricks again. I hope Keith's not after Jane — she's the only new girl I can think of. I'll try and think of a way to remind Eric that he's been warned against that sort of thing before. Indra.

17

From: Aunty Caroline, To: Marshall Winfield

Dear Marshall, I had an email from Stevie asking me for money from the trust fund. Since you normally deal with the fund and I just sign the relevant bits of paper, I was a bit surprised to hear from her directly. I hope you two haven't fallen out? Is there anything I can do to help? We haven't seen you two in ages. I hope you are both well. You must come and visit us. We always have plenty of space — especially in the winter, when the tourists aren't around. I'm sure you could do with a break from all that work and pollution in the city. Uncle Frank sends his love. Aunty Caroline.

From: Marshall, To: Aunty Caroline

Oh dear. Thanks for letting me know. She's lent money to her boyfriend and it seems he's not going to pay it back in a hurry. I'll sort something out. How much did she ask for? Just so that I've got an idea of how much this guy is taking from her. I'm fine. So is Stevie. Hope the B&B side of things is going well and the cows are behaving themselves. We'll try and sort out a time to come visit when it's Stevie's holidays. It would be great to see you again and get some fresh air. Love to you both. Marshall.

From: James, To: Marshall
Explain to me again, on what evidence do you base your theory about Stevie's boyfriend? Jim.

From: Marshall, To: James
He owes Stevie money. Has done for three months. No sign of him paying it back. They came down to London. Stevie paid. They went to a concert. Stevie paid. They had food. I paid. He

looked round the flat with great interest and quizzed me about what it was worth. Stevie is now asking Aunt Caroline to release some money from the trust fund. I've just paid for her car inspection, so I don't know what other expenses she has that her allowance won't cover. All I can think of is that subsidising Buzz is making her spend extra. On a personal level, I dislike the guy anyway. He scorned my *Buffy* collection. Marsh.

From: James, To: Marshall
I scorn your *Buffy* collection.

From: Marshall, To: James
Well, you're ginger. That sort of thing is bound to have repercussions.

From: James, To: Marshall
Tsch. Gingerist comments are beneath you Marshall. Anyway, it may have escaped your notice, but Stevie is a grown up now. She will have to learn grown up lessons by herself. You

can't protect her forever, you know. Much as you'd like to.

From: Marshall, To: James
I know that. But, no matter how old she gets, she'll still be the little kid who used to come to my room in the middle of the night to check that I was still breathing. She was so afraid I'd die too and leave her all alone. I know I should let her make her own mistakes and stop interfering in her life, but I just can't help myself. You'll know what I mean when Molly and the boys are older. Trust me. Marsh.

From: James, To: Marshall
Did she really do that? Jesus, that's the most heartbreaking thing I've ever heard.

Text from: James, To: Louise
Lou, I love you. And I love the kids. I know I don't say it often enough, but I do. Just so you know x

From: Terence Wattley
To: Discipline Subcommittee
Subject: Intra-office relationships

In the matter of the complaint made against Mr Marshall Winfield and Ms Jane Porter. Whilst intra-office relationships, especially between qualified fee earners and trainees, are undesirable from the point of view of company morale and image, there is no real way to prevent such relationships between consenting adults. The best we can hope for is for one of the senior partners to have a word with the offending pair about discretion. In light of the fact that Mr Winfield and Ms Porter have so far conducted their relationship out of office hours and have in no way embarrassed the company, I believe no further action is necessary. However, as Mr Winfield appears to be prone to these liaisons — ref. Ms Dominique DeVale — it should be borne in mind when considering his possible appointment as a partner.

Terry Wattley on behalf of the discipline sub-committee.

From: Human Resources
To: ALL
Memo: On behalf of the partners
Dear everyone,
Staff members are reminded that we are all responsible for the company image. It is expected that everyone will maintain a professional demeanour within the work environment and keep private and professional life appropriately segregated.
Human Resources.

From: Marshall, To: James
Did you see the email from HR? That's the same one they sent out after they hauled me over the coals because of Dominique's theatrics! I'm not sure what to think now. Jane and I have been as discreet as we could possibly be. We barely look at each other when we're at work — which is

not an easy thing to do, incidentally. Yours in shit, Marsh.

From: James, To: Marshall
I did some snooping for you. Rumour has it that our favourite junior partner ratted on you to Susan and Terry. He asked to remain anonymous as he was making an 'informal observation' rather than a formal complaint. He's a nasty piece of work. He REALLY doesn't like you. I'd watch your back if I were you, mate. Have you heard from Terry or discipline committee yet? Jim.

From: Marshall, To: James
No, not heard anything — yet. That's a good thing, I suppose. Although, they're bound to consider it when they discuss the new partners on Wednesday. I hate Keith, I really do. I don't know what I've done to annoy him so much. What a complete git to go to Susan and Terry. And how does he know about me and Jane

anyway??? Marsh.

From: James, To: Marshall
How does he know about you and
Jane? For a clever bloke, you do ask
some stupid questions. He works in
the same team as you. He'd be blind
not to figure out what's going on.
He's probably tried asking Jane out
— like he does with most new blood
around here. She probably turned him
down. I know you and Jane try not to
talk to each other, but the tension
between you when you're in the same
room could cause fires . . . or friction
burns ;-) Jim.

18

From: Keith, To: Susan
Susan, I've just had a call to say my mum's been taken to hospital. I'm going over there as soon as possible. I have an opposition hearing the day after tomorrow, which I obviously will not be able to attend. I shall brief Marshall on it so that he can go in my place. He did some earlier work on the case. I don't think there's anything else urgent. Keith.

From: Susan, To: Keith
That's fine Keith. Take as long as you need. I hope your mother is OK. Susan.

From: Marshall, To: Valerie
Val, can you book me in for flights and overnight accommodation for the hearing in Munich. Details below. If

you can transfer Keith's booking across, so much the better. If you need me, I'll be in Keith's office. M.

★　★　★

Marsh phoned before he went to bed. They had been together almost a week now and already the evening phone calls were the highlight of her night. It meant that she fell asleep thinking about him. It made for very vivid dreams.

When the phone rang, Jane dropped the novel she hadn't been able to concentrate on and pounced on it. Sometimes, she found it funny how excited she got at the thought of talking to him. Had she been this giddy when she'd first got together with Ashby? It was like being a teenager again. It would have been silly, if it wasn't so much fun.

'Hi.' He sounded less upbeat than usual.

'Hello, you. What's the matter?'

'Sorry, is it that obvious? I'm standing in for Keith in Munich. He only briefed me very quickly before he shot off to see his mum, so I've had to read the whole opposition file to get up to speed.' He paused, as though trying to decide whether to carry on with what he was saying.

'And . . . ?'

'And I think I'm going to lose tomorrow.'

'You don't know that. I'm sure it's all in the way you argue it.'

'Normally, yes, but I think our arguments are quite weak. We're claiming they have no inventive step. If the representative for the other side is any good, they'll walk all over us. Keith must be quite glad to get rid of the case.' There was a short silence before he added, 'I'm not suggesting that he would prefer for his mum to be ill, obviously. Just . . . '

'I know what you meant,' said Jane. 'Are you sure it's that bad? What was Keith's feeling on the case?'

'You know what Keith is like. He's all bluster.'

That fitted in neatly with Jane's theory that Keith was over-compensating for his shyness by being gregarious.

'So he thinks you *can* win it.'

'He didn't say that.'

'Well, all you can do is try your best.'

Marsh sighed again. 'You're right. It's just a shame that this happened so close to the partner's meeting. All they're going to remember is that I lost a case.'

'And that you stepped in at the last minute to help out a colleague.'

'Yeah-ah.' He sounded unconvinced.

'Cheer up, Marsh. At least you've got some good news on the stuff you're doing for Susan.'

'Yes, thanks to you.'

'I just got lucky. If I'd taken the second half of that list instead of the first, you'd have found it.'

'And that would have been awful,' he said, with a little laugh.

'Why awful?'

'Well, you wouldn't have got all excited and rushed round to my office . . . '

Jane's mind filled in the blanks. They wouldn't have had that first breathless kiss and things would never have gone anywhere. She would still be wondering if he liked her or not and agonising over how to talk to him. The very memory of that night made her body tingle.

'I wish you were here,' said Marsh, his voice low. 'Right now. In my bed.'

'I know. I wish I was with you too. But you've got an early flight to catch. You should get some sleep.'

'That's true. And if you were here, I certainly wouldn't get that.'

Jane blushed, even though there was no one around to hear. 'Stop it.'

His low laugh made her tingle down to her toes. For one mad moment she considered getting her coat and going across town to his flat. Common sense made her dismiss the idea. 'I'll see you tomorrow.'

'I'll see you tomorrow night. My

flight gets in around eight. Do you want me to come round to your place?'

She still hadn't had him to Polly's flat. Despite how comfortable she felt with him, letting him meet Polly would be a major step. Besides, she had very little privacy at Polly's, whereas they could have Marshall's place all to themselves. 'No. Call me when you're at the airport and I'll head over to yours. I'll even pick up dinner en route.'

'That sounds wonderful. You can help me take my mind off my defeat.'

'Now, now. Be positive.'

'Oh I am positive. You can take my mind off work. Definitely.'

Jane giggled. 'Night-night Marsh.'

'Night, Jane. I . . . miss you.'

'Me too.'

From: Eric, To: Keith
Indra tells me that your mother is unwell. I hope it's nothing serious. Wish her a speedy recovery. Eric.

From: Keith, To: Eric

I'm back in the office today. Too late to go the hearing in Munich. Mum's fine. It was just a ruse to get Marsh to go to the hearing in my place. With him out of the picture, I can spend a bit of quality time with Jane. It was a lousy case anyway. We were bound to lose. This way it'll be Marsh that loses this one. Not me. Bonus. K.

From: Eric, To: Keith
That is low. I know you and Marshall don't get on, but I don't think sabotaging his career is called for. I don't want to be involved in your little shenanigans. The bet is off. I'm pulling out. Eric.

From: Keith, To: Eric
Ha! So, you forfeit the bet. Which means you owe me dinner at the club. Don't come over all straight-laced with me. In my position you'd have done the same. It's called keeping your eye on the prize. Besides, it's

not like I've done Marshall any harm. It'll be a valuable learning experience for him.

*   *   *

Jane was trying to draft a response to an examination report and constantly had to rein in her thoughts as they drifted towards Marshall. She had expected it to be easier for her to concentrate with him out of the office, but it seemed to have the opposite effect. At least when she could hear him next door, she knew where he was. Now, all she could do was daydream.

She was wondering how he was getting on with his opposition hearing when Keith knocked on the door.

'I thought you were at home. How's your mum?'

'She's OK. On the mend,' he said. 'It was a false alarm.'

Ruth looked up from her work. 'That's a relief.'

Keith gave her a quick glance. 'Yes. It

is. Jane, can I speak to you for a moment?' He indicated that she should step outside.

Puzzled, Jane went out into the corridor.

'I was wondering,' Keith said in a low voice. 'Do you fancy a drink after work? I . . . need to talk to someone and you're a friend . . . '

Jane felt a wave of sympathy. For all his bluff exterior, Keith was quite a sweet man at heart. 'Of course. What time?'

'How about I come and get you around five-thirty-ish?'

'That would be fine. I'll see you then.'

'Great!' His voice returned to its normal volume. 'Thanks.'

She couldn't help feeling sorry for Keith. Clearly, his mother's illness had affected him deeply, but he still felt he had to maintain his confident persona. He reminded her a bit of Ashby, who could be feeling dreadful, but would still manage to perform when he needed to. She wished she could be as cool and collected. She tended to show her emotions too easily. She sighed and went back to work.

Her desk phone rang.

'Hi Jane, it's Marsh.'

'Hey. Where are you?'

'I'm still in Munich.' He sounded breathless. 'I won!'

'What? Wow. Well done! I told you you would!' For a moment she forgot that Ruth was in the room and that she and Marsh were keeping their relationship a secret.

'Yeah. The other guy was awful. I don't know where they found him. I can't believe we won. It should have been a complete disaster.'

Ruth's shoulders had stiffened. Her head was still bent over her work, but Jane could tell she was listening. She dropped her voice a little. 'Are you coming back on an earlier flight?'

'No, there isn't one. I've got to kill a few hours. I'm going to see if I can get some work done. I've got to go. I just wanted to tell you the news myself.'

'Thank you. And congratulations!'

'Thanks. I'll speak to you this evening.' She could hear the smile in his voice.

She hung up, and was wondering whether to make something up about the phone call to allay any suspicions Ruth might have, when there was a shout from outside.

Val rushed in. 'He won! He wasn't confident when he left, but he won.' Seeing Ruth's confused expression, she added, 'Marsh just texted me. He won the opposition.'

Not wanting to reveal that Marsh had just phoned to tell her in person, Jane said nothing.

'Yes. Isn't that brilliant! I bet Keith wishes he'd gone after all.'

'I'm sure he'd have gone if he could,' said Jane.

Ruth coughed. Val gave Jane a surprised look. 'Hmm.'

* * *

Keith took Jane to a pub off Fleet Street and found a quiet nook for them to sit in. Jane made herself comfortable while Keith was fetching the drinks. She glanced at her watch. Marshall would be flying over Europe about now. When Keith returned, he placed her glass of white wine in front of her and slid into the seat opposite. He took a sip of his pint and sighed.

'Long day?' said Jane.

'Something like that.'

'Have you heard from your mum today?'

'Yes. She's definitely feeling better.' He ran a hand over his eyes. 'It was quite scary, you know. The ride home that day, when I thought I might never see her again.'

Jane nodded. She had nothing to compare it to but the journey home after realising that Ashby had been lying to her. She had felt broken, as though her life had been cracking from that one bullet-hole revelation outwards, just waiting to shatter. But her pain then would be nothing compared to what Keith had been through when he thought his mother was dying. Unable to think of a suitable response, she reached across the table and laid her hand on his.

He looked at their hands and the corners of his mouth moved upwards, just a bit.

He was grateful for her sympathy, she decided. She gave his hand a squeeze and withdrew hers.

'Thanks,' he said. 'It's nice to stop pretending. I try and keep my personal life away from work. It's not professional otherwise, is it?'

Jane thought about her own predicament. Her private life catching up with her work one was the thing that she dreaded the most. 'I know what you mean.'

Keith contemplated his drink. 'She's a fighter, my mum. I guess you'd have to be to put up with Dad for so many years.' He appeared to be looking at something far away. 'Do you know how they met?'

Jane shook her head.

'She was campaigning for women's rights of some sort and was lobbying my dad, who was already an MP. He was one of the youngest people in the Cabinet. He said he'd support her cause if she slept with him.'

Jane couldn't help being shocked at the mercenary nature of the proposal. 'Didn't that contradict her feminist principles?'

Keith shrugged. 'They've been married for thirty-six years. I guess sometimes it's worth compromising your principles. She's an incredible woman.'

'Sounds like it.' She wondered if all men were programmed to think their mothers were wonderful, regardless of whether they deserved it or not.

As they sat together in a thoughtful silence for a moment, Jane's thoughts wandered towards Marsh. Should she tell him about her conversations with Keith? Marsh, who seemed so reasonable when it came to most things seemed to have a blind spot when it came to Keith. He just saw the bold outer image and refused to believe that there might be a vulnerable human being underneath it all.

Keith's voice interrupted her train of thought. 'Your boyfriend's got a new album out at the moment, hasn't he? That must be hard for you.'

For a fleeting moment Jane thought he was talking about Marsh. Then she realised that the word boyfriend had conjured up Marsh, even though Keith had been talking about Ashby. Yes, she was definitely over Ashby now.

Keith was looking quizzically at her, probably wondering why she was smiling. 'Ashby?' she said. 'He's not my boyfriend. He's my ex.'

'Sorry, I didn't mean — '

'Don't worry about it. Yes, he does have a new album coming out. There are posters all over the place.' Now she knew for certain that some people in the office knew about her famous ex. She wondered if it was everyone, or just a select few who had figured it out.

'That must be hard for you, being reminded of him all the time.'

Jane shrugged. 'I don't really care, so long as I get left alone.'

'Really? Don't you miss the fame?'

'No I don't. I'm a fairly private person, I don't really like being under scrutiny.'

'Wasn't it fun though? At least a bit?'

She'd already thought about it a lot. 'I suppose it was at first. But at some point it stopped being just about the music and people started writing about our lives. It got weird from then on. Ashby became a little bit obsessed with it and we'd have to go to these parties, just to be seen. I never knew when a photographer would try and get a casual shot of me. I had to stop going to the supermarket and start getting the shopping delivered. It was just . . . intrusive.'

'And that's why you moved to London? To get away from the gossip mongers?'

'Yes.'

'But what if they find you again?'

'God, I hope not.'

'Well, a few people at work have figured out who you are.'

'I just hope none of them think it's a good idea to contact the press.' The thought of being stalked by photographers again was too horrible. On the other hand, she was just another girl now, not part of the music scene at all. 'Hopefully everyone's lost interest in me, now that I'm not with Ashby.'

'I bet you could make a lot of money if you sold your story.'

'No thanks. It's not worth it. Honestly.'

Keith looked at her in silence for a moment. 'You're a curious person, Jane Porter,' he said. 'Most people are doing their best to become famous and you're trying to avoid it.'

Jane took another sip of her drink and said nothing. What was there to say?

'I respect that. I hope they leave you

alone.' He stared thoughtfully into the distance. 'It must have been really embarrassing for you, having your private life displayed in public like that. Bad enough finding out the person you loved was cheating on you, but to find out the details at the same time as the tabloid reading public . . . '

'Embarrassing? Try humiliating.' She shuddered at the memory, and realised she hadn't thought about the horror of it all for a few days, not since she started seeing Marshall. But she wasn't surprised to find the fear still there, hidden under the layers of everyday thought.

Keith noticed the shudder. 'I'm sorry, I've upset you. I shouldn't have mentioned it.'

'It's OK. I need to learn to deal with it.'

'Well, it's clearly a raw subject for you.' He met her eyes and smiled. 'What say we stop talking about things that upset us and talk about something else?'

'That sounds like a great idea.'

She was still in the pub when Marshall's text arrived to say that he was at the airport. Her heart sped up immediately. 'Listen Keith, I've got to go. I promised a friend that I'd pop by on the way home.'

'Of course.' He finished off his drink. 'Let me walk you to the station. Don't want you getting mugged again.'

'That's very kind. Thanks.' Why on earth had she found him disagreeable all those nights ago? Perhaps because he had been coming on a bit strong. Now that she'd got to know the real Keith, she felt much more comfortable in his company.

'Jane, if you ever need someone to talk to — about Ashby, or anything else. You know you can come and see me.'

She smiled. 'Thank you,' she said. 'I appreciate that. I really do.'

★ ★ ★

From: Keith, To: Eric
Shame you wussed out on the bet.

Plan B is working like a dream. K.

From: Eric, To: Keith
I hear that Marshall won the opposition. On quite a difficult Inventive Step argument. He's quite the hero around here. Your plan B failed rather spectacularly, I'd say. Eric.

From: Keith, To: Eric
I briefed him thoroughly on my arguments so that he could reproduce them at the hearing. Of course he won. As for my plan B — on the contrary, I've just had a nice cosy chat with Jane. It was most illuminating and has given me a cracking idea for how to proceed. This whole thing is less fun without a wager riding on it, but I shall carry on because I enjoy a challenge. K.

19

In the days that followed, Jane was increasingly under pressure with work. As the deadline for submitting the documents to the client drew nearer Susan, Marsh and Keith all piled work on her. In an attempt not to appear biased, Jane always tried to leave Marsh's work until last, but that usually meant having to stay late to finish it. Although Marsh also worked late most nights, she didn't get much chance to talk to him. Keith, who seemed to keep the same hours as Marsh, kept popping round to see her.

On Tuesday, with the deadline the next day, Jane managed to finish everything she was given a little after six. She fired off several emails, distributing the information to Marsh, Keith and Susan as appropriate and sank back in her chair, rubbing her temples. Her head hurt from reading documents on screen.

In the next office, she could hear the clatter of keys as Marsh typed. Jane hauled herself out of her chair and made her way over.

She knocked lightly on the open door. Marsh looked up.

'I'm done,' she said, as she sagged against the door frame. 'Is there anything else you need?'

Marsh looked at the mess of papers on his desk. 'I don't think so. You've done a sterling job. I don't know how to thank you.'

She immediately thought of a few ways, but decided not to say anything. Marsh caught her eye and the dimple appeared in his cheek. 'I've been neglecting you a bit these past couple of days, haven't I?' he said quietly, too low for anyone but her to hear.

Jane checked over her shoulder. 'That's OK,' she said just as quietly. She wanted desperately to go into his office. His hair was ruffled where he had run his hands through it. She wanted to smooth it down and let her fingers trace his stubbled cheek. But if she did that, she might not be able to stop herself from kissing him.

'You look tired,' she said, in a normal tone.

'I've not been sleeping very well. Things on my mind.' He grinned. 'You know how it is.'

Jane knew she'd blushed. She did, indeed, know how it was.

Somewhere a door slammed. 'I'm going to go home,' she said. 'I'll see you tomorrow.'

Marsh indicated his work. 'I'm going to be stuck here for a while. I'll call you when I'm done. Might be a bit late. Is that OK?'

'And you're still on for dinner tomorrow?'

'Oh yes. Definitely. I'm really looking forward to it,' he said meaningfully.

'Me too.'

* * *

From: James, To: Marshall
Partners' meeting today. I'll be rooting for you. I'll do my best to counterbalance Keith. Try and relax and enjoy the evening. Try not to talk about work. Jim.

From: Marshall, To: James
I'm taking the most beautiful girl in the world out for dinner. I have no intention of thinking about work. Or the partners' meeting. Marsh.

* * *

The atmosphere in the office changed subtly with the partners away. People stopped to chat a little more often. There was more laughter.

Listening to people discuss Marsh's chances, Jane refrained from commenting, in case she let slip more than she intended.

'So,' said Ruth as she and Jane walked back to their office together, 'you've worked with Marsh. What do you think his chances are of becoming a partner?'

The mere mention of Marsh in relation to the word 'partner' made Jane crave chocolate. She had to avoid discussing it in case she let slip more than she realised. 'I don't know how it works here. They didn't have partners where I worked before.'

'I think he deserves it,' Ruth said. 'He bills an awful lot of hours. He's in really early and he leaves really late, from what I've heard.'

'I know.' Immediately realising her mistake, Jane said, 'I mean, I've often been here late at night and he and Keith were here too. So I assumed he always stayed late.'

Ruth gave her a sceptical look. 'O-OK.'

'What time will the partners' meeting finish, d'you think?' she said, hoping to deflect Ruth.

'Sometime after lunch. They always go out for lunch and come back slightly squiffy.'

'Even Susan?' said Jane as she followed Ruth into their office. 'I can't imagine Susan being drunk.'

'Oh, she's funny when she's had a bit,' Ruth said. 'She's normally so severe. She's actually quite nice when she's not in work mode.'

Jane would have to see that before she believed it. She sat down and opened up her email. There was still work to be done.

★ ★ ★

From: Polly, To: Jane
So, have you decided what you're wearing tonight? What sort of a restaurant are you going to? Pol.

From: Jane, To: Polly
No, I haven't decided what to wear yet. He said we were going to an Italian place. It's quite near where we are, so I won't have to go far. I was thinking of wearing one of my work dresses with a nice cardigan instead

of the jacket. All my formal things are still at Mum's. Jane.

From: Polly, To: Jane
I'd offer to lend you something of mine, but everything would be too big for you. You're so lucky you're the same size as you were when we were at school. Come to think of it, I might have some of my old clothes from college stashed away somewhere. We can have a root through those if you want. Pol.

From: Jane, To: Polly
I wasn't too worried about what to wear anyway. It's not the first time we're seeing each other. It's not like I have to wow him.

From: Polly, To: Jane
What are you talking about? You absolutely have to wow him. That's what this dinner is all about! My shift finishes at 4.30. I'll see you when I get home. We'll sort something out.

Have you seen him today? Has he said anything to you?

From: Jane, To: Polly
Seriously, Pol. I don't get the impression that I need to keep up the glamour. I always feel so comfortable around Marsh. It's weird. With Ashby it was fun, but with Marsh it's different. When I'm with him I just feel like everything is right in the world. It's like he FITS. No, I haven't spoken to him yet today. He's keeping a low profile. The partners are supposed to be discussing his nomination to the partnership. I think he's quite nervous about it. He looked tired this morning. It must be a bit weird being here when everyone is discussing your chances of promotion.

From: Polly, To: Jane
So, it's like Ashby was shop bought off the peg and Marsh is made to measure?

From: Jane, To: Polly
Yes. That's exactly what it feels like. It looks good, it feels good. Like it was meant to be. I have to get back to work. I'll see you later. Jane.

20

There was a delay on the underground. By the time Jane got home, it was nearly seven.

Polly was waiting for her. 'About time. Hurry up. You've only got an hour to get ready.'

'Can I have a cup of tea first?'

'I'll have it ready for you when you get out of the shower.'

When Jane emerged Polly was waiting, with a pile of clothes. 'These are all my things from college. Maybe we can find something that fits.'

Jane stared at the mound. 'I'm going out for dinner, not the Grammys.'

Polly ignored her and held up a dress. 'How about this?'

It was dove-grey with elbow-length sleeves and an inverted hemline. There was a delicate black design along the hem.

'I used to wear this with a jacket.' Polly rummaged around.

Jane held the dress up. 'It's beautiful.' She gave it a little shake and it swished gently.

'I know.' Polly continued searching. 'I only wore it twice before I ballooned out of it. I remember Andy's expression when he first saw me in it.' She stared into space for a moment, lost in the memory.

'Are you sure you don't mind me borrowing it?'

Polly returned to the here and now. 'Go try it on. I'll never fit into it again. I'd rather it got worn.'

The dress fitted perfectly, except the neckline was too wide and showed her bra straps. Jane took a few moments to change into a strapless bra. When she returned to the living room, Polly was holding a black beaded jacket.

'Oh, you look incredible.' She gestured for Jane to twirl around. 'That dress never looked so good on me. You've really got the legs for it.'

She handed Jane the jacket and steered her to a mirror.

The dress had a timeless quality about it and set off Jane's slim figure and height beautifully. She lifted her hair and piled it on her head. A few strands escaped and framed her face. Jane smiled. She looked very different from how she used to, in long sweeping gowns — often rented for the evening — and blonde. She rather liked the new Jane.

Polly joined her at the mirror. 'You know, I think dark hair suits you much better than blonde ever did.'

★ ★ ★

When eight o'clock arrived, Jane was sitting on the couch, trying not to fidget. She wasn't nervous about going out with Marsh. After all, she'd seen him almost every day for the past few weeks. But Polly had made such a fuss that she found herself giving extra significance to this, her first real date with him, where he would see her in her finery. Her nerves meant that it had taken her longer than usual to apply her make-up. She even caught herself wishing she could just phone up the stylist who used to do her hair and make-up when she went to big events with Ashby.

At exactly eight there was a knock on the door. Polly sprang to answer it, leaving Jane to stand uncertainly in the middle of the living room.

'Hi,' said Polly. 'You must be Marshall. I'm Polly.'

Marsh stepped into the flat and shook Polly's hand. He was wearing a big overcoat that made his shoulders look broader than usual. Underneath, he was wearing a suit, but with no tie. His shirt, a green one that somehow made his hair and eyes look browner than usual, was open at the neck. This little touch had the effect of making him look laid-back and made Jane think very naughty thoughts.

When Marsh caught sight of her, his

eyes widened. For a moment, he looked completely frozen, as though he'd stopped breathing.

Jane felt a rush of satisfaction at getting such a reaction. 'Hi.'

'Wow! You look . . . amazing.' He seemed to have forgotten Polly was there. His eyes were sparkling when he kissed her cheek.

'Have you heard anything about the partnership?' she said, trying to sound casual.

'I'm not thinking about that this evening.' He offered her his arm.

'You kids have fun,' said Polly.

'It was really nice to meet you, Polly,' Marsh said. 'I've heard a lot about you.'

'Likewise.' Polly gave Jane a quick glance. 'It's nice to put a face to the name.'

'I think we should get going.' Jane steered Marsh out of the door before Polly could embarrass her with any suggestive comments.

★ ★ ★

The restaurant was only a few minutes' walk from the flat, but in a street she hadn't yet explored. It looked chic and upmarket, making Jane grateful she'd borrowed something nice instead of wearing a work dress. She glanced sideways at Marsh. He managed to look formal, yet relaxed at the same time.

He caught her looking at him and squeezed her hand.

Everything about the meal was perfect. The food, the wine, the candlelight. The conscious decision not to talk about work meant that they ended up talking about all manner of things: politics, art, the differences between London and Manchester. Jane was pleased to find that Marsh kept up with current affairs, something Ashby had never managed to do. Even better, she and Marsh agreed on a lot of things.

Jane liked the way his face lit up whenever he looked at her. She loved the way her appearance had struck him speechless; the way he listened to her opinion and considered it before replying; the way her body responded to his kisses.

The more she spent time with Marsh, the more she realised how Ashby had used her. To him, she had been a pretty social decoration and not much else. With Marsh, she felt she had met an intellectual equal. Talking to him made her feel as though she were sparkling.

Before dessert, Jane went to the bathroom to touch up her make-up and check her phone. Predictably, there was a message from Polly.

★　★　★

Text from: Polly, To: Jane
You were right, he IS gorgeous. And the dress works. That was EXACTLY the same expression Andy had when he first saw it. Have a great night. A little jealous.

★　★　★

Jane smiled to herself and turned off her phone. She checked her hair and twisted a few errant strands together so that they fell more neatly around her neck. She reapplied her lip gloss.

The wine had given her a slight glow. Her eyes sparkled. She realised that she was the happiest she'd been in weeks. Contented. As though she'd finally come home.

★   ★   ★

Text from: Louise, To: Marshall
Have a good time on your date and try not to worry about the partner's meeting. Don't do anything Jim wouldn't do! x

Text from: Marshall, To: Louise
Since there isn't much Jim wouldn't do . . . I'm sure I will have a good time, Lou. She's amazing. M.

★   ★   ★

When Jane returned to the table, Marsh was busy texting. She paused before sitting down and watched. He was frowning slightly and chewing his bottom lip in concentration. The candlelight cast soft shadows on his face and gave his hair golden highlights. He looked so handsome and gentle.

With Ashby she had felt merely sexy. With Marsh she felt adored.

Marsh looked up. His face broke into a smile and the dimple appeared. Without looking away, he turned his phone off and put it in his pocket. By the time Jane had slipped into her seat, she knew she had his full attention again.

'So, what do you want to do afterwards?' she said, once dessert had arrived.

The look he gave her told her exactly what was on his mind. Flustered, she looked down at her food.

'We can do anything you want.' Marsh reached across the table and took her hand. 'So long as it's not dancing. I can't dance.'

Jane laughed and met his eyes. At that moment, she knew she loved him. Completely and utterly and without question. The realisation took her breath away. Hot on its heels came a wave of desire.

The gleam in his eyes told her he felt the same.

Ignoring the desserts on the table, Marsh summoned the waiter and signed the check. They retrieved their coats, moving with barely concealed impatience. When Marsh slipped her coat over her shoulders, his thumb brushed her cheek, sending a thrill down her spine.

She climbed the steps up to street level, feeling like she was walking on air. As they stepped out into the street, Marsh slipped his arm around her waist. He kissed her temple. 'Right now,' he whispered, his lips warm against her ear, 'I'm the luckiest man in the world.'

Jane raised her face to his so their lips could meet.

Suddenly, there was a flash and the unmistakable sound of a camera shutter. Jane jumped back, her hand instinctively in front of her face. Marsh's grip seemed to tighten around her waist as he raised his free arm protectively.

The flash went off again, momentarily blinding her. In that instant, she felt as though she was back in Manchester, with photographers camping outside the flat, trying to get a candid shot of her or Ashby. It couldn't be happening again.

Surely they hadn't been stalking her. Perhaps they were just photographing the front of the restaurant. It was probably nothing to do with her.

A woman stuck a small recorder in front of her face. 'Miss Porter, I'm Amber from *Cause Celeb* magazine . . . '

Jane turned and ran. Marsh followed. So did the journalist.

'Miss Porter, can you confirm . . . '

'Go away.' Tears blurred her vision. She could see Marsh keeping up with her whilst trying to flag down a taxi.

'Just a few questions. It'll only take a few minutes.'

The flash went off again.

Jane slowed and covered her face with her arm. Across the road, a taxi spotted them and started to turn round.

Marsh stepped between Jane and the journalist. 'She said she doesn't want to talk to you. Leave her alone.'

'And who are you?'

'None of your business.'

The taxi drew up. Jane gratefully dived in.

'Where to, mate?' The taxi driver said, just as the photographer took another photo. He looked at them in his mirror. 'Here, are you famous?'

'Just drive, please,' said Marsh. He started to give Jane's address.

'Not there,' said Jane. 'I don't want them to know . . . '

Marsh gave her a quick glance and asked the driver to take them to Waterloo station.

They took another cab from Waterloo. Throughout the journey Jane said nothing. The sound of the camera shutter had reopened a flood of memories. Soon after she and Ashby split up, she had returned to their flat to retrieve some of her things, only to find that Ashby's conquest had already been to the tabloids with her story. A photographer had been waiting for Jane, and her tear-streaked face had appeared in a gossip magazine within days.

After that, everywhere she went, she felt hunted by people with cameras. Not just professionals, but kids who pointed their camera phones at her when she went past. For a brief time, she was almost as famous as Ashby.

She had fled to London and now it had followed her here. Tears spilled down her cheeks, and she searched in her bag for a tissue. Marsh, who was still holding her hand, gave it a squeeze. Jane had forgotten he was there. Concern etched his face. He hadn't asked her any questions, merely been there for her, but she knew she would have to explain sooner or later. The thought of it brought fresh tears.

By the time they got back to Polly's building, Jane had stopped crying, but was still feeling fragile. She had started to explain to Marsh, but hadn't got very far. He put an arm round her waist as they took the lift up to Polly's flat. She gratefully put her head on his shoulder.

Rather than hunt through her clutch bag for her keys, Jane knocked. Polly opened the door. She took in Jane's face and looked suspiciously at Marsh. 'What's going on?' She moved aside to let them pass.

'We got accosted by a journalist,' he said as he followed Jane in. He quickly sketched out what had happened outside the restaurant.

Jane kicked off her shoes and sank onto the sofa.

'Oh, Jane,' said Polly. 'How dreadful for you!'

Marsh cleared his throat. 'Why is it dreadful exactly?' He perched on the arm of the sofa, his coat still on. 'I understand it's got something to do with your ex, but . . . ? Unless you don't want to talk about it, of course,' he added quickly. 'That's OK.'

Polly discreetly slipped off to the kitchen, leaving them alone.

Jane could tell he was dying to know. He had been so nice about everything, she felt she owed him at least an explanation. She told him everything, about Ashby, about the other women, everything. Marsh listened, his hands clasped in front of him, his face serious.

When she fell silent, he said, 'So you think that journalist today had something to do with the magazine campaign?'

She nodded, unable to speak.

'And your ex is behind all this?'

'Well, either him or his publicist.'

'You could sue him for harassment.'

284

'We thought of that,' Polly called, from the kitchen. 'But that's even more publicity for him.'

Marsh was silent for a moment. Emotions flitted over his face. Finally, he seemed to reach a decision. 'If I ever meet your ex, I'm going to punch him on the nose.'

He looked so serious, that Jane had to smile.

'That's better.' He leaned forward to kiss her.

Jane sniffed. 'I need a tissue. Excuse me a minute.' She went to the bathroom, knowing Marsh was staring after her.

21

You've reached Marsh's phone. Please leave your name and number and I'll call you back.

'Oh Marsh. Buzz dumped me. He wanted to borrow some more money off me and I said you wouldn't let me and we had this huge row and it was horrible. He got really angry and shouted at me and called me names. You were right. He just wanted money from me. The tragic part is that I really, really liked him, Marsh. I really did. I feel like my heart has been torn in two. I'm so miserable. I don't know what to do.'

You've reached Marshall and Stevie's place. We're not around right now, but leave a message and we'll get right back to you!

'Marsh? Where are you? I've been trying to phone, but your phone's off. Call me. Please, please. I don't know what to do. I don't want to see him again. He scared me.'

★ ★ ★

Jane washed her face. Her reflection looked awful. Her mascara was smudged and her face was puffy from crying. Tears had fallen on Polly's dress and puckered the material. With the make-up gone, her face looked red and raw, a far cry from how she'd looked at the start of the date.

Now that the initial shock had worn off, she felt unutterably tired. Although she was grateful to Marsh for bringing her home, she wanted nothing more than to be left alone. It was a lousy end to a date. She sighed and headed back into the living room.

Marsh was perched on the arm of the

chair with his phone to his ear, still wearing his coat. As she walked in, he made an exasperated sound and hung up. 'No reception,' he said as Polly handed him a cup of coffee.

Marsh looked up and spotted Jane. 'Hey. Feeling better?'

Jane tried to smile. 'A bit.'

'I'll just . . . go do some stuff,' Polly said. 'I'll be in my room, if you need me.' She disappeared down the hall.

'I'm going to head off,' Marsh said. He set his still-full cup down. 'Unless you want me to stay?'

Feeling guilty about not wanting him around, Jane shook her head. 'I'm so sorry.'

'Don't be. You've had a difficult evening. I completely understand.'

'Thank you so much, for everything,' she said. 'I'm sorry I ruined our date.'

'That's OK.' He took her face in his hands. 'I had a good time until those people popped out of the undergrowth.'

'Me too.'

His thumb traced the line of her

cheek. 'You're an incredible woman, Jane. I've never met anyone like you.'

'What, a date who ends up crying all over your shirt and talking about her ex?'

He kissed her, very gently. 'I'll see you tomorrow.'

She nodded into his hands. For a moment, she thought he was going to say something else, but he sighed instead and gave her another kiss on the forehead.

After he left, she wished he'd tried to persuade her to let him stay.

Not wanting to talk to Polly, Jane went to her room and lay on her bed. It was all so unfair. Just as she was getting her life back on track, the ghosts of her past were coming back to haunt her. How had the magazine journalist and the photographer known she would be at that restaurant that night?

She hadn't told anyone but Polly. Could Marsh have let the information slip whilst talking to someone at work? Somehow, she felt that was unlikely.

Marsh was more adamant about keeping work and life separate than she was.

She supposed it was possible that the journalist had seen her go into the restaurant by chance and just waited for her to come out again. It wouldn't be the first time something like that had happened.

$$\star \quad \star \quad \star$$

Text from: Stevie, To: Marsh
Marsh! Where r u? I'm coming home. I don't know wot else 2 do!

Text from: Marsh, To: Stevie
I'm here. Don't panic. Your mobile reception is patchy. Where are you?

Text from: Stevie, To: Marsh
I'm on the train. It's the last train & a bit creepy. I didn't know what else 2 do. Didn't want 2 stay at uni.

Text from: Marsh, To: Stevie

Are you OK? Did he hurt you?

Text from: Stevie, To: Marsh
No, didn't hurt me. Just scared me.
He was so angry when I told him that
u wouldn't let me have any more
money. OMG. You don't think he'll
come and attack u, do u? He knows
where we live.

Text From: Marsh, To Stevie
Calm down. I doubt very much that
he'll do that. Don't worry. I'll come
and get you from the station. I shall
see if I can find a late shop that sells
ice cream. I seem to remember that
helps with a broken heart ;-)

Text from: Stevie, To: Marsh
Ice cream would b lovely. I can't
believe I fell 4 him so completely. He
seemed so nice! & he was so gorgeous and generous.

Text from: Marsh, To: Stevie
I hate to say it, but he was generous

with YOUR money.

Text from: Stevie, To: Marsh
I know. I know. U were right. I should
have listened to u. Thing is, my head
knows I'm better off out of it, but my
heart doesn't agree. I feel so miserable.

Text from: Stevie, To: Marsh
Just realised tonight was ur d8 with
Jane! OMG, I'm so sorry. Is it OK me
coming home? I can c if I can find
somewr else. Maybe u could put me
up in a Travelodge 4 the night.

Text from: Marsh, To: Stevie
Of course it's fine for you to come
home. It'll ALWAYS be fine for you to
come home. Idiot. The date went OK,
but things went a bit weird at the
end. I'll tell you when you get home.

Text from: Stevie, To Marsh
Tell me now. I've got nothing better 2
do sat on this train. Please?

Text from: Marsh, To: Stevie
Dinner was lovely. Jane was lovely
too. All was going well, until we left.
There was a photographer and a journalist waiting outside. Jane went to
pieces. She was crying and shaking.
She tried to explain but ended up
talking about how her ex cheated on
her. From what she said, there's a
magazine harassing her and her ex is
behind it all.

Text from: Stevie, To: Marsh
Were they from *Cause Celeb*? Jane is
the *Cause Celeb* Cause of the month.

Text from: Marsh, To: Stevie
I know that. What I want to know is,
how did they know she was going to
be there? You didn't mention it to
anyone, did you?

Text from: Stevie, To: Marsh
Sorry about the delay. Had 2 move
carriages. A really drunk bloke trying
2 chat me up. NO! I didn't mention it

2 any I. Not even Buzz. Why would I? Who did u tell?

Text From: Marsh, To: Stevie
That's just it. I can't think of anyone. Jim suggested the restaurant, but he wouldn't tell anyone. Neither would Lou. It's a mystery. I've found a 24 hr supermarket. They have Ben & Jerry's. I shall get the biggest tub of Phish Food I can find.

Text From: Stevie, To: Marsh
Phish food? I'm not a baby any more, Marsh! Chunky Monkey, please.

22

Jane was jumpy as she travelled to work the next day, constantly on the lookout for anyone who might work for the press. Having reached work without incident, she stood in the lift, breathing slowly and working to relax her shoulders, which were trying to touch her ears. The office should be safer. The photograph was only taken yesterday. No one would know about it yet.

★　★　★

From: Keith, To: Sally
Have you seen the latest edition of *Cause Celeb*? Came out this morning. Page thirteen. K.

From: Sally, To: Keith
Since when do you read *Cause Celeb*?

From: Keith, To: Sally
You'd be surprised. I'm a man of
hidden shallows ;-)

From: Sally, To: Ruth
Ruth, have you seen today's *Cause
Celeb*? I told you it was the same
Jane Porter. Everyone else seems really
surprised. I told them we figured it
out ages ago.

★   ★   ★

The minute she stepped into reception
at the office, Jane knew something was
up. The receptionist looked up from
what she was reading and hurriedly pulled
a piece of paper across to cover it up.
'Hi,' she said, her voice unnaturally bright.

Jane signed in and started across the
open areas to her office. She was in
later than usual, so most of the desks
were occupied. A group of secretaries
was huddled round a computer screen.
They all went silent when Jane walked
by.

'I got it,' someone said, behind her. Jane turned to see one of the secretaries brandishing a magazine. When she saw Jane she froze in place, her mouth a horrified O. 'Er . . . Hi.'

Surely they couldn't have published the photo so quickly? No, there must be some other explanation. She fled to the sanctuary of her office, sank into her chair and opened up her emails.

Text from: Marsh, To: Jane
Hi Jane, hope you're feeling better today. I'm probably not going to be in until this afternoon. Do you want to meet up after work? Somewhere discreet, of course. Marsh

* * *

It had been sent very early in the morning. Maybe he hadn't been able to sleep either. She wished she were with him. If ever she'd needed a hug, it was now.

She rubbed her burning eyes. The

lack of sleep and her nervous agitation were starting to take its toll. Perhaps another coffee would help. It would mean going past all the whispering gossips, but she felt so awful, it was almost worth it. She was resigned to the fact that her photo was in the magazine. She might as well face it. The whispering wasn't going to go away.

Her quiet life was over. Again.

How had they managed to get the photo in today's edition? Surely it took longer than that to get copy into place. Unless they'd been expecting to get the photo last night.

If the journalist had known for certain that she would be coming out of that restaurant . . .

The realisation hit her like an unexpected snowball in the chest.

Shaken, she pushed herself out of her chair. Gossips be damned. She needed coffee.

As she stood, there was a knock on the door. Without waiting, Keith entered. 'Do you mind if I come in. I'd like to have a word, in private.' He was holding a magazine in his hand and his tone was grave.

Was she in trouble?

He closed the door and pulled Ruth's chair to Jane's desk. 'Here. Have a look at this.'

Jane's New Man! Ashby Devastated!

Cause Celeb cause of the month: Spotted — Jane Porter and her New Man.

Acting on a tip off from a reader, *Cause Celeb*'s very own Amber Jackson tracked down Jane Porter, sought after ex-girlfriend of Ashby Thornton and *Cause Celeb* cause of the month.

Unfortunately for Ashby, it looks like our plea went out too late. Jane was seen smooching with her new boyfriend — pictured below and left. Sources say that Jane's new hunk is patent lawyer, Marshall Winfield.

Friends say Ashby is devastated by the news. 'I'm hoping that Jane will come back to me. I love her and miss her. I know I treated her terribly, but I pray that she can see it in her heart to forgive me,' Ashby told reporters when asked about Jane just last week.

Is Jane right to move on with her life? Is her new love hotter than Ashby? Have your say! Log on to our website and comment.

Reader Poll: Should Jane forgive Ashby and take him back? Voting closes midnight on Saturday.

★   ★   ★

Jane's hand shook as she read the short piece of copy. There was a picture of her and Marsh kissing outside the restaurant and another, less clear, photo of the two of them getting into a taxi. She sank slowly into her chair.

'That edition came out this morning,' said Keith, still using that grave tone.

Jane was too shaken to speak. Her hopes of rebuilding her career in blissful anonymity were shattered. She scanned the article again and noted with relief that they hadn't mentioned where Marsh worked. It wouldn't be too difficult to find out though. His name was on the website, after all.

'At least they didn't mention the firm,' Keith said, as though reading her thoughts. He looked at her intently. 'Are you OK?'

'Yes. I was just . . . ' She rubbed her eyes. 'I was hoping I'd left all of this behind. I didn't think they'd be interested in me once I was away from Ashby.'

'You moved city, you changed your hair colour, your job. You did everything you could.' He sighed. 'I blame myself.'

'Why? What does it have to do with you?'

'I should have warned you. About Marshall.'

'Marshall?'

Keith leaned forward, hands clasped, elbows resting on his knees. 'I didn't want to say anything against a colleague, you know. It's a bit unprofessional. But Marshall is . . . How can I put this? He's not above using people.'

He held up a hand as Jane drew breath to protest. 'No, please, hear me out. There was a trainee here, Dominique De Vale. She and Marshall — '

'I heard about that,' said Jane. She didn't see what it had to do with the current situation. She really needed some caffeine.

'They had . . . have . . . an on/off relationship. From what I've heard, they're off again at the moment and she's recently been seen snogging a footballer. I think Marshall may have done this to get back at her and make her jealous.'

Jane stared at him. That couldn't be true. 'They split up,' she said. 'Over a year ago.'

'Is that what he told you?' He shrugged, as though to indicate scepticism. 'Anyway, I'm pretty sure he told the magazine where you were.'

That didn't sound at all like Marsh. Surely, she had spent enough time with him to know what he was like. She would have known if he was using her . . . Wouldn't she? She reminded herself that Marsh wasn't Ashby. It was Keith's word against Marsh's and she trusted Marsh completely. But she'd trusted Ashby too, once.

'I see he's got you believing exactly what he wants.' Keith stood up. 'I won't waste my time trying to tell you otherwise, but think about it. How else would they know you were going to be at that restaurant last night?'

Jane stared at him. The same question had been bothering her all this time.

Keith patted her hand. 'It's a lot to

take in, I know. If you need someone to talk to, just come and see me.' He walked to the door, where he paused. 'One more thing. He and Dominique didn't split up until last month. As far as I know, her stuff is still in his flat. She's out of the country a lot. She works for a multinational company now. Google her if you don't believe me.' He gave her an apologetic smile. 'I'm sorry you had to find out like this.'

Once Keith had left, Jane turned to her computer and stared numbly at it for what seemed like ages.

★   ★   ★

From: Marshall, To: James
Jim, I won't be in until late this morning. Stevie turned up in the small hours this morning. She and Buzz have split up. I was up all night talking to her and I'm too shattered to function. Am hoping to get a couple of hours' kip before I stagger into the office. Marsh.

From: Marshall, To: Susan
Hi Susan, I'm afraid I won't be in until a bit later than usual today as I've got a small family emergency on my hands. I should be in before lunch though. I will, of course, take the morning off as annual leave. I don't believe I have any urgent deadlines that cannot wait until tomorrow. I am currently proofreading my section of the opposition report. I will get this done and email it to you by this afternoon. Regards, Marshall.

From: Susan, To: Marshall
Fine.

From: James, To: Marshall
Is Stevie OK? She sounded pretty upset when she phoned us in the middle of the night. I'm assuming she got hold of you, seeing as she didn't phone us back. I guess there's not much point asking what happened on your date, if Stevie called and broke it up. Jim.

From: Marshall, To: James
Sorry about the delay in replying. I've had a bit of sleep, but still feel like I've been hit by a train. I'm taking public transport in today. I really can't face running. Stevie's heartbroken. She ate a whole tub of ice cream last night, which is a sure sign that she's upset. I'm surprised she wasn't sick. I think she'll be OK though. I wish I'd been wrong about Buzz, but turns out I wasn't. Date was going really well until we stepped out of the restaurant and found a photographer waiting for us. Jane was extremely upset. She thinks her ex is trying to make her life miserable. I'm not sure I understand it totally. All I know is that it's upsetting Jane and I don't like it. Taking the girl home in tears doesn't really count as a successful date. At least it wasn't my fault she was crying. Marsh.

From: James, To: Marshall
Sounds like things didn't go so well

last night, then. It's a shame I can't tell you anything about the partner's meeting to cheer you up ;-) Jim.

★   ★   ★

Jane was cold. Her mouth was dry and her chest felt hollow. She dropped the magazine she'd been clutching on the table. It fell open to the photo of Marsh kissing her. In the moment before that photo was taken, she had been happy. She had been convinced that she had finally escaped from Ashby's shadow and found love. Now all that was gone. With a groan, she lowered her head to her desk, palms covering her eyes.

Keith's words echoed in her head. Could Marsh have told the reporters where they would be? Was he really seeing her and Dominique at the same time? Could she have been so wrong about him? She didn't want to believe anything Keith had told her, but why would he lie?

Other things crept into her mind.

When she had originally asked Marsh out, he had pushed the date into the following week. And he had checked his phone several times during dinner.

There was clearly a female presence in his flat. The tasteful decorations. The *Cosmo* magazines. The expensive perfume in the bathroom. He had said they belonged to his sister, but what sort of student could afford designer perfume? Even if she could, why would she leave it behind when she went to uni? She would have taken it with her. So, whose was it?

What if Keith was telling the truth and Dominique stayed with him occasionally? Perhaps she kept some things at his place for when she was in London. That could explain why he was always checking his phone.

The to and fro of thoughts was making her head buzz. Ugh. It was no use. No matter how much she wanted to believe that Keith was making it all up for some reason, she had to check. But how?

With a heavy sigh, she pulled her keyboard towards her. If she was going to do this, she may as well make a start. She Googled Dominique De Vale and patent. One link took her to a personnel page of a well-known pharmaceutical company. She found a photo of a woman with dark hair and perfect make-up. Feeling sick, Jane shut down the browser.

More odd incidences that she'd thought nothing of suddenly leapt into her mind. That day when Marsh had cancelled on her with that ridiculous excuse about his sister coming to visit — what if Dominique had called? She remembered how he'd been texting someone when she'd returned to the table in the restaurant. The possibility he might have been texting Dominique while he was dining with her hit her like a physical blow.

The more she thought about it, the more she saw things that might support Keith's accusations. Marsh must have told the reporters where they were going for dinner. Who else would have known?

She remembered how he had been trying to phone someone from Polly's flat last night. He had been quite keen to leave. Maybe he had to talk to the reporter.

Jane felt her energy draining out of her. She lay her head on the desk. She had fallen for him, so quickly and so completely, but everything she'd believed was a lie. First Ashby, now Marsh. How could she have been so foolish?

She heard a door open, and then Marsh's voice, slightly muffled, from the next office.

How dare he! How *dare* he waltz in and act as though nothing had happened? He had made her fall in love with him and then betrayed her. And for what? Petty revenge on his ex — whom he was probably still in love with?

Well, he wasn't going to get away with it. She'd been used by a man before, she was not going to let it happen again.

She stood up so fast that her chair shot out behind her and smacked into the wall. She pushed past a surprised Ruth, who was just entering the office, and marched straight into Marsh's office.

He looked up and smiled, making his dimple flash.

She slammed the door so hard the partition rattled.

Marsh's smile disappeared. 'What's up?'

'What's up?' Jane shoved the magazine in his face. 'This is what's up.'

She waited impatiently while he scanned the article. 'Well? What do you have to say for yourself?'

'It's the photo from last night. That was quick.'

Jane snatched the magazine back. 'You knew how much I wanted to stay out of the magazines. You *knew*. And still you did this!'

'Jane — '

'Well, I hope you enjoy it. I hope they like you so much that they hound you until you can't go anywhere without being followed.'

He opened his mouth, but she cut him off with a raised hand. 'I'm not interested in your slimy excuses. I can't believe I was stupid enough to trust you in the first place. I would have gone on being a fool if Keith hadn't said . . . ' Her eyes filled with burning tears. 'To think I liked you. I genuinely liked you and you . . . You betrayed me.'

Marsh reached out.

Jane stepped back. 'Don't touch me.' Her vision was blurring. 'I wish I'd never met you.' She spun on her heel and marched out.

Ruth was just booting up her computer. 'Jane?'

'I'm going home.' Jane located her coat through a haze of tears. 'I'm not well.'

23

From: James, To: Louise
How am I supposed to know what's going on with Stevie! I've been at work, remember. If you're so worried, why don't you phone the flat and ask her yourself? I've got a couple of deadlines coming up, so I really do have work to do. The commotion that's going on in at the other end of the corridor isn't helping. Jim.

From: James, To: Valerie
Val, did I just see Jane storm past?
She looked like she was crying.
What's going on? Jim.

From: Valerie, To: James
I wish I knew. Marsh just got in. Jane
went in, slammed the door, and
shouted at him. Accused him of
betraying her and said that she

wished she'd never met him, and then stormed out, leaving Marsh standing there like a lemon. Hang on. Where's Marsh going?

From: Valerie, To: Indra
Oh my, what an exciting morning we're having today! First, Jane runs off crying. Then, about two minutes later, Marsh comes past looking like he's about to break something and marches into Keith's office without even knocking. He shuts the door, so Sally and I hang around outside, looking through the glass panel. Anyway, Marsh stands over Keith and accuses him of something, we can't tell what. Then Keith looks at him and laughs. There's some discussion. Marsh is clearly angry, because his shoulders are all bunched up and his fists keep curling and uncurling. Keith is sneering at him and not even getting up from his chair. Then Keith says something and, honest to god, I thought Marsh was going to thump him in the

face. He even drew his arm back and everything. I think Keith thought so too. I mean, Keith's not a small man, but he looked terrified. He actually cowered. But Marsh didn't hit him. He just leaned in really close and said something, jabbing Keith in the chest with a finger. Whatever it was, I think Keith nearly wet himself. I didn't see any more because Marsh came out and I really didn't want to be caught lurking outside the door. Bet you wished you still worked in this office! Val.

From: Indra, To: Valerie
Ooh, it does sound exciting over there. So, do you think it's Jane that Keith and Eric having been plotting over? Eric made me cancel the booking, so I take it that Keith lost the bet. Indra.

From: Valerie, To: Indra
I can't believe that Keith! What a toerag. No wonder Marsh was angry. I

hope this doesn't affect his chances of becoming a partner. At least he didn't hit Keith. That would have been very bad. But all that doesn't explain why Jane shouted at Marsh. Any ideas?
Val.

From: Susan, To: Marshall, Jane, Valerie
What the hell is going on? May I remind you that I'm meeting our client tomorrow, for which I need your report, Marshall.

From: Marshall, To: Susan
I'm sorry, Susan, but it looks like I'll have to take the whole day off. I will make sure the report gets to you by the end of today. Marsh.

From: James, To: Marshall
Are you OK?

From: Marshall, To: James
I'm all right. From what I can gather, fucking Keith has put the knife in. He

told Jane that I told the reporter where we'd be. I knew he was up to something. I wouldn't be surprised if he did it himself. I'm on my way to Jane's, to see if I can make her see that I would never do that to her. I knew how much she wanted to just disappear. I would never sabotage that. To be honest, I'm offended that she believed Keith so readily in the first place.

*   *   *

Jane sat on the underground train, dabbing at her eyes with a tissue. All around her mid-morning travellers ignored each other. No one seemed to notice that she was crying or, if they did, they looked away. Jane was grateful. A kind word would have opened the floodgates all over again.

She felt bruised and defeated. When she made the move to London she had felt as though she was bravely spreading her wings and striking off by herself.

Sure, she'd had to move in with Polly, but that was a short term thing until she found somewhere for herself. And then when she met Marsh, she'd thought she was moving away from her disastrous relationship with Ashby.

Perhaps she'd just moved from dependence on one man to depending on another. How else could she explain how desolate she felt?

She had trusted Marsh. He had seemed so kind and reliable, the polar opposite of Ashby. It had never occurred to her he might hurt her in almost exactly the same way.

Her vision blurred as fresh tears gathered. She brushed them away.

By the time she got home, Jane had stopped crying. She dialled Polly's number, but went straight to answerphone. 'It's Jane,' she said, her voice shaking. 'I've found out who told the magazine. It was Marsh. I'm at home. Call me when you can.'

She felt totally drained. The lack of sleep didn't help. Hoping to clear her head, she made herself a strong coffee. After a couple of sips, she decided she needed something stronger and was looking through Polly's alcohol cupboard when someone knocked.

Jane jumped, knocking over a bottle of Amaretto. Should she pretend she wasn't in?

'Jane?' Even through the door she recognised Marsh's voice.

She stood still, hoping he would think there was no one in and go away.

'Jane, I know you're in there,' he said after a minute. 'I heard you moving around.'

Still she said nothing.

'Please, Jane. I didn't do any of those things Keith said. I swear.'

Feeling as though she no longer had the strength to stand, Jane tiptoed across to the living room and lowered herself onto the sofa.

'I'm not going away. I'm going to wait right here until you talk to me. You can't hide in there forever.' There was a sliding noise as if he had sat down against the door.

After a few minutes she heard the soft clicking of keys. Was he working? Jane shook her head, not sure what annoyed her more — the fact that he was sitting outside waiting for her to open the door, or that he was working whilst doing so.

★ ★ ★

Polly phoned during her lunch hour. Jane grabbed the ringing phone and dashed into her bedroom.

'What happened?' Polly sounded slightly muffled, as though she were speaking through a mouthful of sandwich.

Tears prickled her eyes again, but didn't fall as Jane told her what had happened. She had calmed down now, so only anger remained, burning in her stomach like acid.

Polly listened without interrupting. 'Hmm. And Marsh denies it all?'

'Well he would, wouldn't he? He's

still going out with Dominique and seeing me on the side.'

'Whoa! Is he?' said Polly. 'Are you sure?'

'Yes, Keith told me. It makes sense Pol. He's forever checking his phone and he won't commit to anything without checking his diary.'

'Maybe he's just diary obsessive?'

'What? Even outside of work? He claims he doesn't have a social life, so what's to check?'

'Hmm.' Polly fell silent. 'I'm so sorry, Jane,' she said, eventually. 'He seemed so nice.'

'I know.' Jane lay down on her bed and looked at the little rectangle of ceiling. 'I can't believe I fell for a two-timing rat again. I really must have 'idiot' printed on my forehead.'

'You don't!' said Polly. 'Besides, I liked him too. I encouraged you to go out with him. I'm as much to blame as you.'

Jane gave a derisive laugh. 'I'm a big girl. I didn't have to listen to you. It's all my own stupid fault. Clearly, I've learnt nothing from my experience with Ashby.'

'Oh Jane, don't say that. Listen, I won't be done here for a few hours, but I'll come straight home afterwards and we'll talk. OK?'

Jane wondered whether she should mention the fact that Marsh was outside the flat. She decided not to. After all, by the time Polly got home, he would have got bored and left.

24

From: Stevie, To: Marshall
I've just had a call from Lou. She said
that you threatened to hit that Keith
bloke and then walked out. What's
happened? Are you OK? And if you're
not here and you're not at work,
where are you? Stevie. x

From: Marshall, To: Stevie
I'm sitting in the corridor outside
Jane's apartment. She won't let me in,
but I can hear her moving around
inside. In regards to what happened
— I told you about the photographer
last night. Well, that fucking Keith
has persuaded Jane that I told the
magazine where she was. At least,
that's what I gather from my encoun-
ter with Jane. She shouted at me and
then stormed out of the office before
I could ask her what the hell she was

323

talking about. At first I couldn't figure out why she would think that I'd gone to a magazine, then I realised that Keith must have been working on this for a while. First he complains about me to the discipline committee, then he dumps a weak case on me at the last minute, now this. Well, I lost it a bit. He didn't deny any of it. But he knows I can't prove anything. He seemed to find the whole thing funny. He then said something about Jane which I'm too polite to repeat. I barely stopped myself from smashing his face in. Now I'm sitting in a dimly lit corridor, waiting for her to open the door so that I can explain. Thank goodness the netbook has backlighting. My report is hard enough to read without having to squint at it. M.

From: Stevie, To: Marshall
Oh Marsh! How awful. I never did like Keith. What a total fucker! Netbook? Report? Hang on, are you working??? Stevie.

From: Marshall, To: Stevie
Of course I'm working. I've got to keep my billing hours up. And I have a deadline to meet. I don't know why I'm bothering though. I've probably buggered up my chances of promotion for good now. Apart from the whole making a scene in the office thing, I nearly hit a colleague. I'm sure the partners will take a very dim view of that sort of thing. Great. I've ballsed up my career and my love life in one morning. Fabulous.

From: Terence, To: Susan
Susan, what the hell is going on with your staff? Keith has just made an official complaint against Marshall. Apparently, he threatened to hit him but, as far as I can gather, didn't actually hit him — Keith was a little evasive on this point. I can't ignore this, obviously. Terry.

From: Susan, To: Terence
I doubt Marshall would have attacked

Keith for no reason. Heaven knows, I've been tempted to hit Keith myself a few times. Let me find out what's going on before you launch an official investigation. I'll talk to their respective secretaries and see if they can shed some light onto the situation. Susan.

From: Terence, To: All Staff
Subject: Mr Marshall Winfield and Mr Keith Durridge. Both of the aforementioned will be suspended pending investigation of certain allegations. The door-code has been changed. The investigation will be carried out by Susan Jameson and Alison Sallet.
Terry Wattley on behalf of the partners.

From: James, To: Marshall
Fwd: Mr Marshall Winfield and Mr Keith Durridge
Have you seen this?

From: Marshall, To: James

Yeah. I've just seen it. Bang goes my promotion then. Never mind. I'm past caring, to be honest. If I can just talk to Jane and sort all of this out, I'll be happy. Although if I knew I'd get into this much trouble, I would have actually punched Keith. My life would still be ruined, but at least I would have had the satisfaction that he would need new teeth. Marshall.

From: James, To: Marshall
Stevie says that you're sitting outside Jane's apartment? Is this true? Man, you must have it bad. I'll do what I can for you at this end. Jim.

From: Marshall, To: James
What can I say? I love her. I realise that now more than ever. I still can't believe she'd take Keith's word over mine. M.

From: Jane, To: Ashby
My job is in jeopardy, my relationship with Marsh is a mess. My life is

totally destroyed. I hope you're happy.
Jane.

From: Ashby, To: Mike
Dude. Had an email from Jane. She's
really upset. I didn't realise your plan
would mess with her personal life so
much. Any chance we could call this
off? Ashby.

From: Mike, To: Ashby
I explained the strategy to you and you
agreed with it at the time. Too late to
call it off now. Besides, it's working.
Have you seen Twitter? Everyone is
talking about you. And your album
will be out next week. The timing is
perfect, even though I say so myself!
Now, you let me worry about the publicity and you guys concentrate on
what you do best! Make music.

From: Pete, To: Mike
Call off the hounds or we go public
about it all being a gimmick. Pete,
Josh, Lee and Ashby. PS: We mean it.

25

Jane crept up to the door and peered through the spyhole. She couldn't see anything. Just as she was about to retreat again, Marsh's head popped up.

'I thought I heard you walking.' His face was distorted by the spyhole.

Jane knew he couldn't actually see her. 'Go away.'

'Not until you talk to me.'

'No.'

'Well,' he said, 'you don't actually have to open the door for me to talk to you.'

Jane put her fingers in her ears. She could hear muffled sounds of Marsh talking as she walked back to her room, but couldn't make out the words. Fine. There was nothing he could say that could make this better.

★   ★   ★

Text from: Stevie, To: Marsh
How r u getting on? Any progress?

Text from: Marsh, To: Stevie
No progress. She won't open the door
or even talk to me through it. I really,
REALLY need coffee, but I can't leave
here.

Text from: Stevie, To: Marsh
Why don't u call up the local café
and see if they'll deliver one?

Text from: Marsh, To: Stevie
Don't be ridiculous. Can you imagine
the conversation? 'Where would you
like it delivered to?' 'The corridor outside flat 32, please.' 'Flat 32, got it.'
'No, the corridor outside. Oh, and
there's no point buzzing to be let in,
she won't let you in. You need to ask
the guy at the desk to send you up to
the floor . . . ' No, I think I'll have to
remain caffeine-less for now.

Text from: Stevie, To: Marshall

How did u get in, if she didn't buzz u in?

Text from: Marsh, To: Stevie
I followed someone else in. I just have to hope she's not so cross that she calls security.

From: Stevie, To: Valerie
Val, have you got an email address or phone number for Jane Porter? Marsh is sitting outside her flat, trying to talk to her and she's not letting him in. He's had about two hours sleep and only one cup of coffee. Things could go horribly wrong if someone doesn't do something. Love Stevie.

From: Valerie, To: Stevie
I only have her work email address: JPorter@ramsdeanandtooze.comm. I'll see if I can get any more info from HR. Strictly speaking, I'm not supposed to divulge this sort of information. Val.

From: Stevie, To: Jane

Hi Jane. My name's Stevie Winfield.
I'm Marsh's sister. I don't know if you
can pick up your work emails from
home. Marsh told me what happened.
I just wanted to say that he would
NEVER do what you accused him of.
Let me tell you about my brother.
When my parents died, I was thirteen
and he was twenty-one. He became
my legal guardian. Rather than give
up uni, he bought the flat for us to
live in, and he studied, did up the flat
and looked after me all at the same
time. He became my mum and dad
and my best friend as well as my
brother. Any semblance of normality I
have in my life is because of him.
Does that sound like the sort of man
who would betray the girl he loves,
just to get his face in the paper? Also,
his career was the only part of his life
that he felt like he had any control
over and he threw himself into it. It
means the world to him. Trust me, I
know. There is NO WAY he would

jeopardise this promotion by doing something like this. I understand that you got your information from Keith. He's a sleazebag and not above lying and cheating. He made a pass at me when I was seventeen. I wouldn't believe a word he says. That's all, really. Marsh loves you. He wouldn't do anything to hurt you. Stevie xxxx

★ ★ ★

Jane was stalking around the flat, trying to ignore the fact that Marsh was still on the other side of the front door. If she stood still and listened, she could hear the soft tip-tap of his fingers on the keyboard. An image of him, sitting hunched up on the floor, working, floated into her mind. She shook her head and turned on the TV. Loud.

It was odd, knowing he was out there. It was almost like it was before, when she had been trapped in the flat, unable to go out because of people lying in wait for her outside. At least she wasn't frightened of Marsh. Angry, yes, but not frightened. She tried to concentrate on what was on telly. At some point in the middle of *Murder She Wrote*, she fell asleep.

The sound of voices in the corridor woke her. Marsh was talking to someone. Jane hit the mute button on the TV and listened. Polly's voice. She heard them talk back and forth, and then Polly's key grated in the lock. She sprang to her feet and spun round to face the door.

Polly smiled at her apologetically. 'I think there's someone here wanting to talk to you.' She stepped aside to let Marsh through.

Ever since her conversation with Keith, Jane had been seething about Marsh and what he'd done. In her mind, she'd painted him as two-faced and evil. But the Marsh who shuffled in, still stuffing his computer into his bag, looked anything but evil. His hair was a mess, there were bags under his eyes and his suit was crumpled, just as though he'd been sitting on the floor in it.

Completely against her better judgement, Jane felt the urge to throw her arms around him when he gave her a tentative smile.

She remembered why she was angry and pulled herself together. 'I have nothing to say to you.'

'Hear me out,' he said.

Behind him, Polly slipped away to her room.

Jane crossed her arms. 'Fine.'

'I didn't do it. All that stuff you accused me of, I didn't do any of it.'

'Of course you're going to deny it. You'd be stupid not to.' Whatever else she could call him, she knew he wasn't stupid.

'But Jane, why would I do it? I knew you wanted to be left alone. What possible reason would I have to tell the press where you are?'

Her anger reignited. 'How should I know how your twisted mind works? Maybe you just wanted your face in the papers? Or to tell everyone you'd slept with a famous bird.' The minute she said it, she wondered if that was true. Her stomach twisted with disgust at the thought.

Marsh's face was a picture of horror. 'That's just ridiculous. I can't believe you'd even think that.'

'And what about Dominique?'

'What about Dominique?' He looked genuinely puzzled. 'What does she have to do with anything?'

'Oh, so you deny that you two are still together?'

'Oh course I bloody deny it! We split up ages ago.' His frown was turning into a glare. He was losing his calm, but she didn't care.

'Who lives with you in your flat then?'

'My sister. Stevie.'

'Oh yeah? What about the perfume?'

He stared. 'What bloody perfume?'

'Aha!'

'For heaven's sake!' He reached in his bag, tore a corner off a protruding piece of paper and scribbled something down. 'Here. She's there now. Call her.'

Jane didn't move.

Marsh let the paper drop. He stepped closer and his eyes flashed with anger. 'Look, you insane woman, Keith is lying. He wanted to stitch me up. It was probably him that told the magazine in the first place.'

Jane backed away. 'Why on earth would Keith lie? What does he have to gain?'

'You don't know the guy.' His tone was bitter.

'You're right. I don't know him any more than I know you.'

'And yet you trust his word over mine?'

When Jane didn't respond, he went on. 'I knew it was a mistake to fall for you. Before I met you, I was set to be promoted. Now, thanks to all this, I'll be lucky to have a job tomorrow. And you know what? Until five minutes ago, I would have thought it was worth it.

'I would have thrown away the job of

my dreams and started over, just to be with you.' His mouth twisted down at the corners. 'And it turns out that you don't even trust me enough to stand up for me when Keith spins you a ridiculous yarn. I can't believe I was so stupid!' He glared at her, hurt and resentment etched on his face.

All the fight suddenly drained out of her, leaving her close to tears again. 'I don't know who to believe any more.'

The anger in his eyes subsided. 'Perhaps that's something you need to work out for yourself. I'm just sorry I got involved.'

He turned and walked out, shutting the door behind him.

26

Text from: Marsh, To: Stevie
Am coming home. Make coffee.

Text from: Stevie, To: Marsh
Oh dear. Guess things didn't go well
then. I will have coffee ready. And
I've just been out 2 get more ice
cream. Chunky Monkey OK 4 u?

Text from: Marsh, To: Stevie Thanks
:-)

Text from: Stevie, To: Marsh
Ur welcome. Us Winfield kids should
stick 2gether, right? X

★　★　★

Jane stared at the door for minutes after
Marsh left.
　'Well, that didn't go so well,' said

Polly, making Jane jump.

Her thoughts were a jumble of hurt and anger. The piece of paper with Marsh's phone number lay at her feet. She picked it up.

'For what it's worth, I believe him,' Polly said.

'I don't know, Polly. I'd like to, but who else would have known where we were going for dinner?'

'God, he could have mentioned it to anyone.'

'I don't think he did. He was always very keen on keeping everything hush hush. Which is why it makes sense that he's probably still got a girlfriend. I mean, there's clearly a woman living in that flat from time to time.' She waved a hand, as if gesturing at a shelf full of cosmetics. 'There's *Cosmo* magazines and cellulite scrub and everything.'

'Maybe it is his sister's, like he said.'

Jane sank into a chair. 'Maybe.'

'Look, why don't you call the flat and find out. He said she was there at the moment.'

Jane looked at the paper. 'What if it's Dominique and she pretends to be his sister?'

'So phone and ask for Dominique then. If it's her, she'll say so, won't she?'

'I guess.'

Polly thrust the phone at her. 'Go on. Do it before he gets home.'

To her surprise, her hands were shaking as Jane punched out the numbers. She took a deep breath and put the receiver to her ear.

'Hello.' A female voice.

'Uh . . . ' Her throat had gone dry.

'Hello?'

'Is Dominique there, please?'

There was a short silence. 'Who is this?' the woman said on the other end. When Jane didn't reply, she continued, her tone frosty. 'Dominique doesn't live here. She never has. I don't know where she is, so I can't take a message.'

'Oh. Can I ask who I'm speaking to, please?'

'This is Stevie Winfield. Who are you?'

Not knowing what to say, Jane hung up.

'Well?' said Polly, who was perched on the end of the sofa.

'She said she was Stevie Winfield.' Jane looked at the number on the paper. It was a London number, but that was all she could really deduce from it. 'It might not have been the number to his flat. He had hours to cook something up. He could have asked Dominique to pretend to be Stevie . . . '

Polly made a disgusted noise and rolled her eyes. 'I give up! If you won't help yourself, then there's no point me even trying. You really have to let go of this Ashby thing, Jane. If you don't, you'll end up sabotaging every single relationship you have. Just because Ashby was a rat bag doesn't mean Marsh is, too. Until you get that into your head, you're never going to be happy.'

27

From: Marshall, To: Susan
Hi Susan, The finalised report, as
promised. Let me know if you need
anything else. Marshall.

From: Stevie, To: Louise
He's just texted to say he's coming
home. Apparently, it didn't go well. I
can't believe she took Keith's word
over Marsh's. What a moron.

From: Louise, To: Stevie
Keith can be very persuasive and
charming when he wants to be. It
comes from having no scruples what-
soever. Jim says both Marsh and Keith
have been suspended. Apparently,
most people have a lot of sympathy
for Marsh. Not surprising really, I'm
sure most people would love to have
the chance to thump Keith. Poor

Marsh. It's the first time in years that I've seen/heard him get worked up about anything that wasn't about you or work. He lets his heart start beating again, only to have it stomped on.

From: Stevie, To: Louise
I hope he's not going to be down in the dumps for ages. I hate leaving him by himself when he's depressed, but I do have to go back to college.

From: Louise, To: Stevie
He won't be. It didn't take him long to recover from Dominique.

From: Stevie, To: Louise
I think this might be different. He wasn't in love with Dominique, even though he probably thought he was in the beginning. I think he was almost relieved when they split up. I don't think he was that surprised to find out she was cheating on him. He was just embarrassed about the scene she made. He really liked Jane. You

should have seen his face when he talked about her. It would have made me puke if it wasn't so sweet.

From: Louise, To: James
Jim, I'm worried about Marsh and Stevie. Is there anything we could do to help, do you think? On the plus side, Marsh's predicament seems to have made Stevie forget how heartbroken she was over Buzz. Also, please don't forget that you've got to pick Molly up from the childminder at lunchtime tomorrow. I'm going to the Natural History Museum with the twins' class, remember?

From: James, To: Louise
I won't forget Molly. What sort of a father do you take me for? I've set a reminder on my phone. I don't see what we can do for Marsh and Stevie. I'm doing my best to get Marsh off the hook in the office, but there's only so much I can do. I don't think he's going to make it to partner this

time round, which is a real pisser because they'd already decided to promote him. If only he'd postponed his bust up by another half a day, they would have announced it! I don't know what else we can do for them, aside from being there if they need a shoulder to cry on. Don't worry. Those two are tough. They've been through worse together and come out relatively normal. Love Jim.

From: Susan, To: Eric
Come and see me tomorrow. 9.25. Susan.

From: Eric, To: Keith
Why did you have to drag me into this? I've just been summoned to talk to the partners about your little run in with Marshall.

From: Keith, To: Eric
Relax. I'll take care of it. We're partners. Marshall is not. Disciplining partners would look bad. K man.

From Stevie, To: Aunty Caroline
Hi Aunty Caroline, I know it's short notice, but can Marsh and I come down to you for the weekend? We're both suffering from broken hearts at the moment and could do with cheering up a bit. Yes, Marsh had a new girlfriend! A nice one this time, not like Dominique. I hope they can get things sorted out and they get back together. I've never seen him quite so loved up as he was when he was with her. Would it be OK for us to come tomorrow? We'd help with the farm and the B&B and things, obviously. Love Stevie.

From: Aunty Caroline, To: Stevie
Hello Stevie darling. Of course it's OK for you to come and stay for the weekend. You can stay for longer if you'd like. There aren't many tourists around at the moment since it's winter, so we're not that busy with the B&B. I'll get two rooms ready for you and Marshall. I'll have to bump

two of our regulars up from single to double rooms, but that's not a problem. It'll be lovely to see you both. I'm sorry to hear you're both suffering from broken hearts. I'll have to bake you a nice cake to cheer you up. Love Aunty Caroline and Uncle Frank.

Text from: Stevie, To: Marsh
FYI: When u get back from moping around in coffee shop, we r going 2 c Aunty Caroline for the weekend. I've persuaded her 2 make 1 of her cakes 2 cheer us up. No need 2 thank me!

Text from: Marsh, To: Stevie
Hang on. I can't just take off like that. Especially on a weekday. And I'm not moping. I'm working.

Text from: Stevie, To: Marsh
I thought u were suspended from work. It's not like you'll be going in anyway!

Text from: Marsh, To: Stevie

There's no mobile reception at Aunty C's place. I won't know it if they do want me to come in! It does sound tempting though. I'll call Susan and see what she says.

From: Marshall, To: James, Louise
Stevie and I are heading to Wales to see our Aunty Caroline for the weekend. We should be back by Monday. I've spoken to Susan and she agrees that it's most unlikely I'll be asked back into the office tomorrow anyway, so I may as well go away. Mobile reception at Aunty C's is pretty awful, so don't expect much communication from me — or Stevie, Lou! I'll check email each night though. Hopefully, I'll see you on Monday, Jim. Marsh.

From: James, To: Marshall
Is Aunty Caroline the one who used to send those fantastic cakes? You lucky bugger.

28

At around five on Friday morning, Jane gave up trying to sleep and dragged herself out of bed. She made herself a coffee and sat on the sofa wondering what to do.

She missed Marsh. It hurt so much to think she could never hold him again that she wanted to forgive him.

No, she told herself. That was a stupid idea. She had let her heart rule her head with Ashby and look how that had ended. She had to accept the evidence. No one but Marsh had known about the booking at the restaurant.

She blew her nose. Splitting up with Ashby had hurt a lot. But that was nothing compared to how miserable she was now. She dreaded seeing Marsh when she went to work. It would be really hard to remain objective. And it would all be so horribly public.

He would probably try to talk her round. There was a risk she might give in and forgive him, only to be devastated when he betrayed her again.

To make things worse, everyone would be talking about her. The magazine article, all the stuff about her and Ashby, her very loud argument with Marsh, had all been discussed. They would all be waiting to see how she was dealing with it.

What had Marsh meant about possibly not having a job tomorrow? Had something else happened that she didn't know about? Was she out of a job too?

She couldn't access work emails from Polly's, so the only way she could find out was to phone someone. But she didn't know anyone well enough to phone them up at five in the morning. She would just have to wait until she got into work.

Her head throbbed and her eyes burned. Her nose and throat were swollen and raw. All she really wanted was to go home to her mother. But she'd run away before, and it hadn't made any difference.

London hadn't been a refuge. She'd just spent her time looking over her shoulder and jumping at shadows. Then, just when she had started to believe that the gossip columns had forgotten about her, the paparazzi had turned up. She hadn't escaped her past.

Perhaps Polly was right. The only way to deal with it was to accept it.

The first step was to go to work. Jane sighed and drained her coffee. Since there were still several hours to go before she needed to leave the house, she might as well have a good long bath.

*   *   *

Cause Celeb Blog

Ashby Thornton's rival in love

Ashby Thornton's ex-girlfriend, Jane Porter has a new boyfriend, but who is he? *Cause Celeb's* Amber Jackson finds out.

Jane's new hottie is Marshall Winfield, a patent lawyer specialising in chemistry, at London patent law firm Ramsdean and Tooze. Good-looking and brainy too! Jane met Marshall when she fled Manchester to hide away from her heartbreak at losing Ashby. Is this just a rebound romance, or have Jane and Marshall discovered a chemistry of their very own? Look for a detailed exclusive in next week's issue!

* * *

Thankfully no one else was waiting for the lift. Jane used the few seconds of solitude to gather her thoughts.

On the underground journey in, she had worried that everyone would stare at her, but no one had paid her any attention.

London was big and impersonal enough for her to go about in peace. But work was a different matter. She wasn't just a nameless face in the crowd. The office gossip network would have been busy so it was fair to assume everyone had seen the article and photograph. It would be pointless to pretend it had never happened. Her insides trembled at the thought of facing everyone, but she didn't have much choice.

The doors pinged. Jane drew a deep breath and stepped out. Pleasance, the receptionist looked up from behind the glass doors. She looked a little frazzled.

'Morning, Jane. Feeling better today?'

'Morning.' Jane forced a smile. 'Yes, thanks. I think I've got over the shock a bit now.'

'We all knew ages ago, you know.'

'And I thought I was doing such a good job keeping a low profile.' Jane hoped her tone sounded light.

'To be fair,' said Pleasance, 'it was only news because they made such a fuss about you disappearing in the first place. That really backfired on you, eh?'

'Looks like it.'

The phone rang. 'Good morning, Ramsdean and Tooze.' Pleasance frowned, her eyes flicked to Jane. 'May I know who's calling please?' She listened for a moment, the corners of her mouth tightening. 'Could you be more specific, sir? Perhaps, the name of your company?' A slight nod. 'Yes. Why don't you do that? Goodbye.' She hung up and sucked her teeth. 'They have been calling all morning. Ever since they found out where you work. Every other call is for you or Marsh.'

Jane sighed. 'I'm sorry.'

'Just as well Marsh isn't coming in today.'

Jane's chest clenched from a mixture of disappointment and relief. 'Why? Where is he?'

Pleasance gave her a funny look. 'You should know.'

Of course, people thought they were still together. Jane shook her head.

'Oh.' Pleasance's expression went from surprise to concern. 'What happened?'

Jane shrugged. 'It's complicated.'

'Have you two had an argument? Is that why he hit Keith?'

'What?' She couldn't imagine Marsh hitting anyone. But then, she hadn't thought he'd be the sort of person to talk to the press either. Obviously she was a terrible judge of character.

'Of course. You left early and missed all the excitement. It was quite incredible.' Pleasance's eyes flicked to someone behind Jane. 'Wasn't it, Ruth?'

'What was?' said Ruth, as she unfurled a long scarf from around her neck.

'Marsh punching Keith in the face.'

'He didn't actually punch Keith. Nearly did, though. That's what Val said.'

Pleasance's reply was cut short by the phone ringing again.

Ruth laid a hand on Jane's arm. 'Come on. I'll fill you in on what happened.'

As she followed Ruth through the office, conversations stopped and eyes tracked their progress across the floor. Jane could feel the hairs on the back of her neck stand on end. She hated being stared at. It made her feel exposed and vulnerable. She focused on the back of Ruth's head and walked on, being careful not to look at anyone.

Once they were in their office, Ruth gave her an account of the previous day's excitement.

'And what happened afterwards?' She imagined there would be repercussions. People weren't allowed to go around threatening to hit other people in law firms.

'They're both suspended. Susan's interviewing people to get to the bottom of it all and then the partners will decide what action to take.'

Suspended! The Marsh she knew would have been devastated by that.

But, she reminded herself, she didn't really know him that well.

Her head was starting to hurt again. She rubbed her temples.

She'd thought Keith was pleasant, if a little misunderstood. She'd seen Marsh as shy and, basically, a nice man. It was hard to believe that either of them would sell her story to a newspaper.

She wanted to believe Keith was lying and Marsh was in the clear, but try as she might, she couldn't think of a single motive for Keith to talk to the magazine. His name was never mentioned, so he couldn't be doing it for publicity. He might have been paid, but she doubted *Cause Celeb* was that desperate to know her whereabouts. It wasn't that big a story, surely. The only one who had anything to gain was Marsh.

'Jane,' said Ruth. 'Are you OK?'

'It's just . . . so hard to believe that either of them could do this.'

'Surely, you don't still suspect Marsh

told the magazine?' Ruth said.

'Well, I can't see who else did.'

'Marsh would never do that. Especially not to someone he was going out with.'

Jane bit her lip. It was no longer a secret that she and Marsh were seeing each other. After all, it was all over the gossip press. But she hadn't realised he'd talked about her to Ruth.

'Oh come on,' said Ruth. 'I know you and Marsh did your best to keep it a secret, but it was really obvious. You went red whenever he came in, and he couldn't keep his eyes off you. It was all quite funny, really. You guys were trying so hard to be nonchalant that it just made it all the more obvious.'

'Right,' said Jane, barely above a whisper. She opened her email. There were several messages waiting for her. One was from an unfamiliar address: StevieNoWonder. Spam that had got through the office filter, probably. She moved her mouse to delete it just as her reminders pinged. She flicked to her calendar.

'Seriously, Jane. There's something you should know.' Ruth leaned forward. 'Val said — '

'I've got a meeting with Susan. In two minutes!' She looked up at Ruth, feeling slightly panicked. 'Why does she want to talk to me?'

'She's doing the investigation into what happened.' Ruth shrugged. 'She interviewed me about it yesterday. It makes sense that she'll want to talk to you. You're a key player in the whole drama.'

'I'd better go then.' Jane shot to her feet. She was already in trouble. She didn't want to be late as well.

Susan and another woman were sitting in the office when Jane knocked. 'Come in, Jane. Sit down.' Susan indicated a chair across the desk. 'This is Alison, from the regional office.'

Alison, who was small and matronly and looked out of place in a suit, shook Jane's hand and gave her a warm smile.

The tension in her shoulders slackened slightly. She sat down.

Susan leaned back and steepled her fingers. 'Jane, as you probably already know, I'm trying to find out the truth about the assault that Marshall is alleged to have made on Keith yesterday morning. I gather you're a key part of this, so can you tell me, in your own words, what happened yesterday.'

Jane outlined what she knew, including what had happened the night before. From their expressions, she could tell that none of it was news to Alison and Susan. When she had finished, there was a short silence while Susan made notes.

While she waited, Jane's worries about her position resurfaced. She was, after all, still on her probationary period. 'Am I in trouble?' she blurted.

Susan looked up, frowning. 'I'm not exactly pleased. But I do understand that all of this is not really your fault. You seem to have done your best to avoid being in the papers.'

Jane felt a great weight lift off her shoulders. 'Thank you.'

'However,' said Susan. 'You should have told us about this situation when we interviewed you.'

'It didn't seem relevant at the time,' said Jane. Remembering where she was, she added, 'I thought you might not give me the job if you knew.'

Susan raised an eyebrow. 'You underestimate yourself Jane. But, I suppose it didn't seem that relevant at the time, since you hoped you had escaped. However, when this wretched *Cause Celeb* campaign started, you should have mentioned your concerns.'

She waved Jane's attempt to speak aside. 'It doesn't matter now. What's done is done. We will work out how best to manage it. I have emailed you a list of journal articles that I need. I'd appreciate it if you can get copies to me by lunchtime, so that I can read them before I meet the client.'

Susan's change of tack confused Jane for a moment. 'Er . . . OK.' Unsure whether she was dismissed, she looked at Alison, who gave her a small nod. Before she reached the door, Susan called her name. She turned back.

Susan was tidying papers on her desk. 'Marshall Winfield is an exceptional young man, with maturity far beyond his years,' she said. She looked up briefly and then back at her papers. 'The same cannot be said for Keith Durridge.'

Jane almost ran to the Ladies. She needed a moment of privacy to sort her thoughts. Susan's last comment had taken her by surprise. Had she said to believe Marsh and not Keith?

The only thing that pointed to Marsh telling the press was her assumption that no one else knew where they were going for dinner. What if that assumption was wrong?

Locking herself into a cubicle, she sat down on the closed lid and buried her face in her hands. Right now she didn't want to talk to anyone. The only person she really wanted to see was Marsh.

The intensity with which she missed him surprised her. It wasn't just that she missed his touch, she missed having him to talk to. In the few weeks she'd known him, she had been more comfortable than she'd thought possible. He had been more than just her lover. She had genuinely felt as though she'd met her soul mate.

Tears escaped and ran onto her fingers. She wanted to believe that Marsh was the man she'd fallen in love with, not the conniving weasel that Keith suggested. But did she want it badly enough to be made a fool of all over again?

She rubbed the tears away and took a deep breath. She couldn't fall apart at work. Standing, she dabbed away the last of her tears and straightened her jacket.

Jane had to pass Jim Edwards' office on the way to hers. Jim and Marsh were old friends. Had Marsh told Jim where he was taking her? Could Jim have inadvertently told the press?

Hope rose inside her chest. She backtracked a few steps.

Jim looked up when she entered. He didn't look surprised to see her. 'How can I help you?'

Relieved that she didn't have to explain why she was there, Jane said, 'Did Marsh tell you where we were going for dinner?'

'Yes, but I didn't tell the press, if that's what you mean.'

He had a friendly, open face. She believed him. 'I didn't think you would have.'

'Are you OK? Do you . . . want to talk about it?'

For a moment, the genuine concern in his voice nearly undid Jane. There was something reassuring about Jim. Just as there had been with Marsh. Right now, she would like nothing better than to sink into a chair and let someone look after her. But this wasn't the time. She shook her head.

'Probably just as well,' said Jim. 'I

couldn't have promised you confidentiality anyway. My wife would have tortured the information out of me.'

Jane forced a smile. 'She's a good friend of Marsh's, isn't she? He mentioned her.'

'She's very protective of him,' he said. 'We both are. Listen, I won't tell you what to think about Marsh. If you didn't believe him, you won't believe me either. But I will tell you that you're wrong about Keith. You might want to talk to Val, or any of the other ladies in the office, about him and his past exploits.'

Not knowing how to answer, Jane said, 'Oh.'

'And please believe that Marsh's feelings for you were genuine. He's as upset about the photo as you are.'

'It didn't look like it on the night,' said Jane. 'He couldn't wait to leave the flat.'

'That'll be because Stevie had been trying to call him all night to tell him that she'd split up with the boyfriend and was coming home. His phone was off, so she kept leaving messages.' As though reading scepticism in her expression, he added, 'I know, because she phoned us in the middle of the night too.'

Stevie again. His sister seemed to be Marsh's alibi for everything.

Jim seemed to sense that there was nothing more to say. 'Anyway, I'm sure you've got things to think about. If you do want to talk about it, or just hide, consider my office yours.'

'Thanks.' Jane took a step backwards. 'I should go . . . '

On the way back to her office, Jane wondered whether she believed Jim. He was Marsh's best friend and could just be telling her what Marsh wanted her to hear. On the other hand, she found it hard to believe he would do that. She had liked him instinctively when she'd first met him. Just like she'd liked Marsh.

She felt a surge of sadness as she thought about her first meeting with

Marsh, that tiny spark of interest had been the first sign that she was recovering from her experience with Ashby. Even in that brief conversation, when he was just a jogger who'd bumped into her, she'd liked him.

How could something that felt so right go so horribly wrong?

She thought back to her first impression of Keith. He had made her uneasy. She'd thought he was a shark. But over time his interactions with her had disarmed her and she had grown to like him. Maybe her first impression had been the more accurate?

She paused outside Marsh's office. In the adjacent bay, Val had her headphones on and was typing up dictation notes. When she looked up, Jane turned to move on.

Suddenly, the image of Keith looking at something on Marsh's desk flashed into her mind. He had shut the desk diary as Jane walked in.

Marsh wrote everything down. He'd said so.

She practically ran into the office, which was in semi-darkness. The diary lay on the table where it always did. Jane went to it and started flicking through.

Someone switched on the lights. Jane looked up to see Val standing in the doorway, her arms crossed.

'Are you looking for something?' she said. 'I have a pretty good idea of Marsh's filing methods, I can probably tell you where to look.'

Jane ignored her. She had found the page. In neat letters, Marsh had written the time, the name of the restaurant, the phone number, 'dinner with J' and 'booked in the name of Winfield'. If Keith had seen the page, he would have known exactly where they were going and when. 'Keith knew.'

'Knew what?' Val said. 'That you were going out with Marsh? I hate to break it to you, but everyone knew that.'

Ordinarily, the comment would have made Jane blush, but she was too excited to even notice at that moment. 'No, he knew we'd be at the restaurant at that time.' Her thoughts were tumbling over each other in their haste to be first. 'So, he could have told the magazine. But why? Why would he do that?'

'Ah,' said Val. 'I think I might be able to help you with that. You . . . might want to sit down.'

Jane lowered herself into Marsh's chair. It seemed strange to think that he sat in it day after day. The seat was uneven, as though it was moulded to fit his body. She waited expectantly.

Val appeared uncomfortable, but she quickly outlined the details of Keith's old bets with Eric and what she knew of the new bet. When she came to the end, she said 'Are you OK? You've gone pale.'

For the second time in forty-eight hours, Jane felt her world spin. Emotions wrestled each other and fury won. How *dare* Keith treat her like that!

Her first instincts about him had been right. He had engineered all the rest to fit his aim of bedding her before Marsh did. When he failed at that, he set about trying to sabotage their relationship, just to get at Marsh.

And it had worked. Not only had Jane done exactly what Keith expected her to do, but Marsh had responded by confronting Keith and got himself suspended from work, ruining his chances of becoming a partner.

'Poor Marsh. I was so awful to him. I'll call him. I must apologise.'

'I think that would be a good idea,' Val said, relief evident in her voice.

Jane got the impression that Val was rather protective of Marsh too.

Back in her office, Jane sank into her chair. Absent-mindedly, she opened her email. That spam message was still there. She highlighted it and hit delete.

As the message disappeared, Jane's brain suddenly made a connection. Stevie. That was Marshall's sister's name. After a flash of panic, she retrieved it from her deleted items folder.

What she read made her cry.

29

It took a few minutes for Jane to compose herself enough to phone Marsh. After all, what could she say to him? Sorry didn't even begin to cover how she felt. Her unfair accusation must have hurt him deeply. Polly was right. She was still hung up on what Ashby had done and was using it to sabotage her relationship with Marsh.

She ducked into an empty meeting room, took a deep breath and punched in Marsh's number. The call immediately went to answerphone. 'You've reached Marshall Winfield's mobile. Please leave your name and number and I'll call you back.'

She stared at the phone for a moment. Just hearing his voice, even in the form of a recorded message, brought home to her the enormity of what she'd thrown away. Tears prickled at her eyes. She had to see him. As soon as possible.

Jane hurried back to his office, not quite running. 'Val, do you have Marsh's number at the flat?'

'Sure.' Val opened her drawer and pulled out a black notebook. 'But he's not there.'

'Where is he then?'

'He and Stevie have gone to Wales to see their aunt,' said Val. 'Do you still want the number for the flat?'

'Um . . . Do you have a number for his aunt's place?'

'No, I'm afraid I don't. Have you tried his mobile?'

'It's off.'

'You could see if Jim knows.'

Jim was in a meeting, so Jane spent an agonising hour in her office, half-heartedly ordering papers for Susan and getting up every so often to see if Jim was back. Every moment of delay felt like an eternity. The longer Marsh went on believing that she didn't trust him, the worse things got.

When she'd finally ordered the last paper, she emailed Polly.

* * *

Text from: Jane, To: Polly
I've really blown it this time! I've figured out how Keith knew where we were going for dinner on Wednesday. You know how I said I couldn't think of a single motive for him to talk to the press. Well I was wrong. It turns out that he had some sort of bet with Eric in the regional office that he would sleep with me. How sickening is that? I'm glad he's not here. I feel dirty just thinking about being in the same building as him. It's disgusting. The really sickening thing is that, in a world full of unreliable, despicable men, I found one that was nice and I let him slip through my fingers. I'm such an idiot Pol. I wish I were dead.

Text from: Polly, To: Jane
Woah, that's a long text. You must be

upset! I told you Marsh seemed like a good guy! So, you made a mistake. You were distraught and made a rash judgement. It happens. Why don't you call him and apologise. I'm sure he'll come round. Hugs.

Text from: Jane, To: Polly
I tried to call him, but his mobile's off. Apparently, he's gone to visit his aunt in Wales. I'm hoping Jim will have contact details for the aunt, but he's been in a meeting for the last hour. I'm going mad with impatience.

★   ★   ★

The instant Jim was back in his office, Jane rushed over. 'Do you have the phone number for Marsh's aunt's place?'

'Does this mean you've decided to believe him?'

'Yes, I want to apologise,' said Jane, impatient to get on with it. 'Val says he's gone to visit his aunt and you might have the number.'

'I'm afraid I don't know it off hand. But I can ask my wife.' He held up a finger. 'Just a sec.' He picked up the phone and started tapping in the number but then paused, frowned and put the receiver back. 'I've just remembered she's on a school trip with the twins. Her phone's switched off. They must be inside the museum.'

Her feelings must have shown on her face because Jim said, 'I'm sorry. I'll try and think of any other information that might be useful. His aunt owns a B&B on a working farm. I can't remember what it was called but my wife . . . ' He stopped, looked at his watch. 'Oh, shit.'

'What?'

'I'm supposed to be looking after my daughter this afternoon.' He started shoving papers into his briefcase. 'I'm sorry Jane, I've got to go. I promise I'll call if Lou or I think of anything, OK?'

'Ok.' She turned to leave, her heart now sunk into her shoes.

'You could email him. He checks his

email every night.'

'Thanks. Have fun with your daughter.' She couldn't wait until the evening to speak to Marsh.

★   ★   ★

Text from: James, To: Louise
Do you have Marsh's aunt's phone number?

Text from: Louise, To: James
Why the hell would I have Marsh's aunt's phone number? More importantly, DO YOU HAVE MOLLY?

Text From: James, To: Louise
Of course I have Molly. We're turning a cardboard box into a boat at the moment. As if I'd forget to pick up my daughter. Lou, you wound me.

Text from: Louise, To: James
I'm sorry Jim. I should have more faith in you. Marsh's aunt's B&B is somewhere near Abergavenny. Her

name's Caroline, the uncle's name is Frank. The place probably has a website. Try Google. Gotta go. I left the kids with a teacher while I popped to the loo. Best get back. They're having a great time, by the way. The dinosaur is a hit. Lou. xxx

From: Terence, To: The Senior Partners
In the light of Susan and Alison's investigation, it is recommended that both Marshall and Keith be allowed back to work with a warning. As it appears Keith has been reprimanded for something similar before, and considering he caused enough provocation to precipitate Marshall's actions, I suggest he is made to account for his actions before the partners' committee. I believe a written warning may be called for, at the very least. As this matter is currently part of the company gossip, it is probably inadvisable to make Marshall a partner yet. I suggest we wait until the furore has died down and promote

him following the next meeting. We have decided to leave the decision on what to do about the trainee, Jane Porter, up to her supervisor — who, in this case, is Susan. On a personal note, I just hope no one brings the company name up in the newspapers. Terry.

★　★　★

Even though Jane did her best to concentrate on her work, she kept thinking about Marsh all afternoon. The memory of the hurt on his face just before he left her flat kept coming back to her. How could she have been so wrong?

It was late when Jim finally called. 'Bad news, I'm afraid. We don't have a number for Marsh's aunt. All we know is that the B&B is near Abergavenny.'

Jane scribbled down everything he said. 'Do you know their surname?'

'No, sorry.' There was a scream in the background. Jim said, 'Just a minute sweetheart, Daddy's on the phone. I'm sorry we can't be more help. Like I said, you can always email him and ask him to call you.'

'I'll see what I can find,' said Jane. 'Thanks for all your help.'

'Glad to help. I hope you catch him.' There was renewed screaming in the background. 'I'd better go. Good luck.'

The internet gave Jane three possible B&Bs in the right area, but she couldn't narrow it down any further. She wrote down the numbers for all of them and tapped the end of her pen on her notepad.

'You could try phoning the local tourist information office,' suggested Ruth.

'They're not likely to know, are they? I don't have a surname for Caroline and Frank.'

'How about just phone up and say 'Is Caroline there?' They'll say if it's a wrong number,' said Val, who had come in with some files and was hovering.

Jane looked up, her mood suddenly

lighter. 'That's doable. I'll use the phone in Marsh's office, if that's OK. I need to concentrate.'

Val had clearly been hoping to help. 'Yes,' she said, sounding disappointed. 'I guess you'd want some privacy.'

The first number she tried rang for ages, but no one answered. A woman answered her next call almost immediately.

'Is Caroline or Frank there please?' Jane crossed her fingers.

'I think you've got the wrong B&B, love.'

'Oh, sorry to have bothered you.' Jane hung up quickly and crossed the number off her list. She dialled the last one.

The phone rang and rang. Jane frowned. Honestly, you'd think they'd at least have an answerphone. Something simple like 'this is Caroline, leave a message' would have sufficed. She was about to hang up when someone picked up mid ring.

A man cleared his throat. 'Hello

'. . . er . . . White Cottage B&B.'

The sound of Marsh's voice struck Jane like a physical blow. She hadn't been expecting to hear it and suddenly, she found herself unable to speak.

'Hello?' said Marsh again. He gave a sigh. 'They hung up,' he said to someone in the background. A second later there was a click and he was gone.

Jane stared at the receiver in her hand. She was shaking. Slowly she cradled it and sank into the chair. Hearing Marsh's voice had driven home to her how much she wanted to see him.

All she had to do was dial the number again and talk to him, but somehow talking to him wasn't enough. She couldn't possibly apologise over the phone for the massive injustice she'd done him.

She had to see him. She wanted to see his face and gauge his mood. Her fingers curled round the armrest of his chair.

She needed to be able to touch him.

30

It started to rain shortly before the train reached Jane's stop. By the time she got off, the water was being whipped sideways by the wind and running in ribbons off the station roof. Suddenly the journey seemed less like a good idea. The night was dark and cold, and she hadn't reserved anywhere to stay.

What if Marsh's aunt didn't have room in her B&B? Besides, if things didn't go well with Marsh, she wouldn't want to stay there anyway. Wouldn't it have been more sensible to phone up and talk to Marsh beforehand? Instead, she'd rushed headlong into the journey, without thinking about the consequences. Of course, if she'd followed her heart in the first place, she wouldn't be in this mess.

'Are you all right, love?' A station

guard seemed concerned. 'Can I help you?'

Jane started. 'I need to get to this B&B.' She showed him the information she'd printed from the B&B's website.

'Ah, that'll be Frank and Caroline's place,' he said in a sing-song accent. 'That's funny though. They normally come pick people up if they're this late.'

'I wasn't expecting to be this late,' said Jane. 'Is there a taxi rank near here?'

'Not at the station, no. You'll have to phone for one. Tell you what love,' he said, kindly. 'You sit in the waiting room and I'll call one for you.'

'Thank you.' She sank onto a wooden bench and hugged her small bag. Now, sitting in a cold train station in Wales, she realised how tired she was. She had barely slept since the photographer had jumped out at her two days before. Today she'd rushed home after work and thrown a few things into an overnight bag before practically running to the station.

She shivered. It was colder here than in London. She wished she'd packed a thicker jumper. The hems of her jeans were wet. All she wanted right now was to curl up and go to sleep. The last of her energy reserves drained away, and she rested her head on top of her bag.

The station guard touched her shoulder, waking her up. 'Your taxi's here, love. Get you to the B&B. You look like you could do with a warm bed.'

Gratefully, Jane stood up, her limbs protesting. 'Thank you so much.' It seemed like a long time since a stranger had been so kind to her.

'Oh don't mention it,' he said. 'I have a daughter your age. I'd like to think people are nice to her when she needs it.' He shooed her out towards the exit, where a taxi was indeed waiting.

* * *

The taxi left Jane in front of the B&B. The sound of its departing wheels crunching on the gravel was soon swallowed up by the sound of the rain. Jane stood still, getting increasingly wet, staring at the white house. A light above the sign shone on wet ivy leaves and gleamed on the stone doorstep. Even in the pouring rain, the house looked inviting.

From inside came a burst of laughter. Clearly the B&B had guests, maybe even a full house. She gathered her courage. It was too late to turn back now. If she did, she might as well give up on Marsh forever.

Taking a deep breath, she tried the door. It was open.

Somewhere off to the right she heard voices. A notice on a shelf saying *Reception* sat next to a bell. After a moment's hesitation, Jane rang it.

A woman appeared, wiping her hands on an apron. She was tall and thin, with a crop of blonde curls. 'Hello. Can I help?'

'I need a room?' It was meant to be a statement, but it came out like a

386

question. She had been so busy thinking about what to say to Marsh that she hadn't really thought about this bit. But she did need a room.

'Of course,' said the woman. She looked Jane up and down. 'You poor thing, you're soaking. Come through. It's warmer in here.' She opened a door and shooed Jane ahead of her. 'I'm Caroline.'

They entered a large room with a small bar at one side. In front of the fire crackling in the hearth, two middle-aged women in walking clothes were sitting in arm chairs. They were chatting with a young woman who was sitting on a floor cushion with her feet stretched out towards the fire. Everyone looked towards Jane.

The young woman had dark hair pulled back into a pony tail. When she smiled a dimple appeared on her cheek. Jane knew she was looking at Marsh's sister.

She smiled back and murmured a greeting, glad that the rain plastered hair and lack of make-up made her anonymous.

Caroline went behind the bar and pulled out a book. 'Can you fill in your details here, please?'

Behind her the three women resumed their conversation. 'So why does she think he told the magazine?'

Jane froze, halfway through writing her address.

'I dunno. Paranoia?' From the tone of her voice, Jane could tell Stevie wasn't well disposed towards her.

'I must admit, it doesn't seem like the sort of thing he would do,' said the other woman. 'Mind you, I don't know your brother at all.'

Her companion chuckled. 'You've only just met him Isabel.'

'Yes, but you get a feeling about a person, don't you?'

Jane signed her name. Yes, you got a feeling about a person. Her feeling about Marsh was that he was a good man. She should have trusted that feeling. Instead she had let her bad memories of Ashby interfere and ruin a perfectly good relationship.

'I'm afraid both the single rooms have been taken,' said Caroline. 'I've got a double you could have.'

'That will be fine.' Feeling she ought to add something more, she said. 'It'll be nice to have room to stretch out.' Her jeans were starting to stick to her legs and she was cold. She would very much have liked to go and stand by the fire, but she wanted to hear the rest of the conversation.

'So, what's he going to do?' said Isabel.

'His boss is going to decide that and let him know on Sunday.'

'I didn't mean about that. I meant about his girlfriend.'

'Oh,' said Stevie. 'I don't know. But, if she can't believe him when he says he didn't do it, he's better off without her.'

'Maybe she just made a mistake.'

'Hmph. He is really miserable.' Stevie sighed. 'I think he really liked her.'

Caroline handed Jane a key. 'Breakfast is seven-thirty until nine. I usually cook it to order, so if you tell me what you want, I can have it ready for you.'

Behind her, Stevie said, 'It's so annoying. It's been ages since he's liked someone, and he finally lets himself fall in love and this happens. That woman doesn't know what she's let go of.'

Jane almost turned round to point out that she did know what she'd let go of. Difficult as it was to listen to herself being described in less than sympathetic terms, she felt she somehow deserved it. She had been so stupid. She had been rehearsing what she was going to say all the way from London, but now it seemed horribly inadequate.

The door opened, letting in a blast of cold air, and Marsh stepped into the room. He was wearing a dripping waterproof and his arms were full of small logs. He spotted Jane as soon as he entered and froze in place, as if he couldn't believe his eyes. After a moment he arranged his face into a carefully neutral expression, as though he was waiting to hear what she said before deciding how he felt.

Out of the corner of her eye, she saw Stevie straighten up and knew she had been recognised.

Jane managed a weak smile. 'Hi.'

'What are you doing here?' He sounded perplexed, but not particularly angry.

'I . . . ' She took a quick glance round the room. Stevie was getting to her feet. Everyone was looking at her. 'I came to find you.'

'Why?' He was still clutching the bundle of logs like a shield. Water dripped off his hood and fell on his nose. He twitched his head, making the hood slide off. When the firelight caught his features, Jane suddenly longed to see him smile.

Stevie went to his side, her face set as though she was preparing to defend her brother.

Jane had hoped to talk to Marsh in private, but it looked like that wasn't going to happen. She took a deep breath. 'I'm sorry,' she said. 'I was wrong. I know that. I should have believed you from the start. I should have known you'd never say anything to the press.'

Marsh's expression remained carefully neutral. He said, 'Yes, you should.'

'I know. I think at some level, I did know. But I let my memories of Ashby cloud my judgement.'

'I'm not Ashby.'

'I know that too. I didn't mean to compare you to him. It was all just such a shock that I jumped to conclusions. I'm sorry Marsh. I'm really, really sorry. I don't know what I can say that would make things better between us.'

'What changed your mind?'

'I really couldn't believe you'd told *Cause Celeb* where we'd be, but the evidence . . . Then I figured out who else could have known we'd be there.' She blinked back tears that were blurring her view of him. 'I was so wrong, Marsh. I needed to see you and apologise as soon as possible, so I came here.'

He continued to stare at her, coldly impassive.

She had expected some reaction from him. 'Please, please know that I'm very sorry. I've never met anyone like you before. You were so perfect and we were good together . . . But I was so scared of getting hurt again that I let you slip through my fingers. I'm a very stupid person.' She brushed a tear away. 'If you never want to see me again, I'll understand, but for what it's worth, I love you.'

The silence in the room was broken only by the cracking and popping of the fire. Everyone seemed to have lost the ability to move.

Jane held her breath.

'Well, she sounds sorry to me,' Isabel said, making everyone jump.

Marsh glanced at Stevie and a look passed between them. Without a word, he handed her the bundle of logs.

With two long strides he was across

the room. 'I'm not Ashby, Jane. And I would never take you for granted the way he did.' He looked into her eyes. 'All I ask is that you do the same for me.'

Jane nodded, trying to inject all the sincerity she felt into that small movement. When Marsh smiled, she felt her heart swell with relief and love.

He took her face in his hands and kissed her.

For a moment she forgot the world around her. All she knew was the pressure of his lips and the warmth of his hands. She felt insubstantial, as though the only thing holding her up was him.

'Aaaah,' said one of the ladies. 'If only that were part of the service, you'd get a lot more custom, Caroline.'

Marsh drew back slightly, his eyes shining. 'I've made you soaking wet.' He stepped back, releasing her.

'Oh no, I was like that when I came in . . .'

'You poor girl.' Caroline appeared

beside her. 'Marshall, why don't you show Jane her room and then come back down. I'll have a sandwich and a mug of hot chocolate waiting for you to take up.'

'You don't have to do that,' said Jane.

'Nonsense,' Caroline said. 'You must be freezing cold and shattered if you came straight from work. Go on Marshall, before the poor girl catches her death of cold.'

Marsh grinned and picked up the key Caroline was brandishing. He took Jane's hand and led her out of the room.

'I feel like I should give them a round of applause,' said one the ladies. Everyone laughed.

★ ★ ★

The room was quaint in a traditional B&B sort of way. The duvet bloomed with pink rosebuds and a china bowl sat on the dressing table. As far as Jane was concerned though, the best thing in it was Marsh.

'You should take a hot shower.' he said. 'I'll go get this tray that Aunty Caroline's threatening you with.'

Jane had been too nervous to eat more than a couple of biscuits on the train. Now she realised she was actually quite hungry. A shower sounded lovely too. She felt dirty and sticky from having been at work all day and then on a train for several hours. Much as she wanted to grab hold of Marsh and never let go, she feared he would find her icky in her current state. 'Promise you'll still be here when I come out?'

Marsh put his arms around her and held her. 'I can easily promise that.' He kissed her just below her ear, sending a thrill of pleasure down her side. 'Besides, those ladies down there would hunt me down and beat me with their walking boots if I ran away now.'

★   ★   ★

The shower made Jane feel much better. By the time she emerged, dressed in a large T-shirt and a jumper that wasn't warm enough, Marsh was sitting on her bed with a tray containing two steaming mugs of hot chocolate, a chicken sandwich and two slices of cake.

'You're lucky,' he said. 'Not everyone gets a slice of cake.'

As she settled down to eat, Marsh sat behind her and put his arms around her. 'So, what happened at work?'

'Oh Marsh, I'm so sorry about your promotion.'

'It's not your fault. It was bloody Keith. Anyway, tell me what happened.'

She leaned against him and, between mouthfuls, outlined what was going on.

'Hmm.' He rested his cheek lightly on the top of her head. 'Doesn't sound good, does it?' His sigh made the hairs on her nape stand up.

'Susan's on your side,' she said.

'I know. She's a scary boss, but very loyal to her staff,' said Marsh. 'Besides, I get the impression she knows what Keith's like.'

'Maybe he tried to pull something on her when he first started,' said Jane. They both sat in silence for a moment, contemplating it.

'Nah,' Marsh said after a moment. 'Not even Keith is that stupid.' He looked over her shoulder. 'Are you done?' He slid off the bed and set the tray on the dresser. When he returned to her and gathered her to him in a kiss, Jane flung her arms around him and kissed him back.

They lay together on the bed, kissing with the enthusiasm of teenagers. After some time, Marsh said, 'I guess I should tuck you in and take that tray downstairs.'

Jane groaned. 'Do you have to?'

'I think I should. I don't think I'm allowed to sleep with the paying guests.' He paused and shuddered slightly. 'Not that I've ever wanted to before.'

Jane slipped under the duvet. Marsh tucked her in. 'It gets quite cold at night. Are you sure you're going to be warm enough?'

'I would be if you were in here with me.' Her eyes were already closing.

'I'll see what I can do.' He kissed her forehead. 'Goodnight, Jane. Thanks for coming to find me.'

'The pleasure was all mine,' she whispered.

★   ★   ★

Jane woke in the middle of the night, wondering where she was. Remembering, she smiled into the darkness. Marsh loved her. OK, she was in the tabloids again and her job was in jeopardy, but she could deal with all that. Because Marsh loved her.

There was a soft knock on the door. Jane sat bolt upright, her heart suddenly leaping with hope. 'Yes?' she whispered, and turned on the bedside lamp.

'It's Marsh,' came an answering whisper.

Jane slipped out of bed and opened the door. It was cold now that she was out of her nice warm bed. She let Marsh in and scrambled back under the duvet.

He was barefoot and wearing jeans and a T-shirt. In the soft light of the bedside lamp, he looked ruffled and unutterably sexy. 'Do you still need a hot water bottle?'

Suddenly Jane was very much awake. 'It is quite cold.'

'Certainly is.'

She enjoyed the movement of muscles as he pulled his T-shirt over his head and dropped it on the floor. Jeans and boxer shorts followed soon after. Jane had to resist the urge to reach out and grab him.

'Shift up,' he said.

'No way. I've warmed this side of the bed up. I'm not moving.'

Marsh slid in between her and the duvet. His naked body pressed against hers.

Jane's heart sped up as she felt his heat. He propped himself up on his elbows so that he didn't crush her. 'In that case,' he said, as he traced the line of her jaw with his finger, 'we'll just have to share.'

31

From: James, To: Marshall
Welcome back. It's good to have you around again. I see Keith is back too. Never mind. Were the committee fair to you? I gather not being made partner is your punishment. I suppose that's punishment enough, really. Jim.

From: Marshall, To: James
I'm just grateful to have my job. I guess we've all been let off lightly. Of course, none of it was actually my fault. Or Jane's. Susan hinted that strong words have been had with Keith. She wouldn't be drawn any further on that. I'd better get back to work. The client has OK'd the text we sent, so I have to finalise the documents and get them filed before the deadline. Marsh.

From: Marshall, To: James
PS: Thanks for helping Jane out when she was looking for me.

From: James, To: Marshall
That's what friends are for. Lou wants you and Jane to come for dinner and tell her all the details. She says you owe us. Jim.

From: Marshall, To: Louise, Cc: Jane, James
Lou, Jim says you want to feed me and Jane. How about weekend after next — Stevie will be back down for the weekend. She's still a bit cut up about Buzz, but seems to be coping OK. Marsh.

From: Louise, To: Marshall
Excellent. I'm looking forward to meeting Jane, we've heard so much about her. It will be lovely to see Stevie too. I spoke to Stevie yesterday, in fact. All she wanted to talk about was you and Jane. I guess it's taken

her mind off Buzz nicely. I'm really happy that you've found someone. I've always said it was a waste that you were single. Love Lou.

32

Cause Celeb Exclusive Interview: In conversation with Triphoppers

Nearly eight months after the release of their fabulous second album *Swagger!* the boys are taking a well-earned break from touring. Ashby, Pete, Lee and Josh talk to our very own Amber Jackson about life on the road, food, sleepless nights and the search for love.

The interview will be available to download as a podcast so that you can listen to it over and over again!

What are the questions you've been dying to ask them? Email your questions to Amber and you might even hear the answers.

From: Human Resources, To: All Staff
Subject: Keith Durridge
Keith Durridge will be leaving Ramsdean and Tooze to take up a position as head of patents at the soap manufacturer SolTol International. Keith has been with R&T for fifteen years, since he joined us as a trainee. We congratulate Keith and wish him well in his new venture. Keith's last day will be Thursday. A presentation will take place in the canteen at 12.30. Gerry Bently, Human Resources.

From: Susan, To: All Staff
Subject: New Partners
On behalf of the partners, we would like to congratulate Marshall Winfield and Georgina Heath on being nominated to become partners of Ramsdean and Tooze. There will be doughnuts and tea to celebrate on Friday.

Jane hummed to herself as she walked towards the music megastore, where she'd meet Marsh before they went to Jim and Louise's for dinner. The sun was shining on streets still slick with the morning's rain. Traffic hissed over wet tarmac. She was snug in her winter coat and was feeling warmer and happier than she remembered ever being.

As she passed the entrance, she saw a large cut-out of Ashby and the band. Once it would have caused her a twinge of hurt, but now she felt nothing. She didn't even bother to read what it was advertising, and went straight upstairs.

Marsh was frowning as he looked through a row of CDs. He looked round when she spoke and smiled. 'Hi,' he said, and gave her a quick kiss.

'What are you getting?'

He showed her a handful of CDs. 'It's been ages since I bought any new music. I'm looking for the band Stevie keeps talking about.' He flicked through more CDs. 'Ah. Here we are.'

'*The Electric Beehives*,' Jane read over his shoulder. 'What do they do?'

'Heaven knows. Apparently, they're indescribable.' Marsh did a good impression of his sister showing awe.

Jane chuckled. 'That could mean anything.'

When Marsh had paid for his purchases, he looked at his watch. 'We've still got loads of time. Fancy a coffee?'

The coffee shop on the top floor was full of excited teenaged girls. Jane and Marsh found a nice alcove and sat squashed together, drinking their coffee and taking wild guesses what 'indescribable' might possibly describe. Suddenly all the teenagers stampeded out of the coffee shop.

'Wonder what's going on.' Jane's voice sounded loud in the suddenly empty room.

'A band's doing a signing today,' said a waitress as she picked up half empty cups. 'It's always like this when there's a signing on. Chaos to start with and then they all run off, leaving half eaten stuff everywhere.' She threw a barely touched muffin into a bin bag.

'Perhaps we should get out while the exits are still visible,' said Marsh.

'I'd use the side entrance, if I were you,' said the waitress. 'The bands are usually at the front end of the store.'

The upper floors were deserted and there was a huge racket coming from downstairs. As they walked to the escalator, Jane looked over the side and saw screaming fans waving pieces of paper and clothing at a group of people who were being moved through the crowd by big men in suits.

'I wonder who it is.' The moment the words left her mouth, she recognised the band. In the same instant, Ashby looked up. He stopped, making Pete, the drummer, walk into the back of him. The rest of the band looked up too. One by one, everyone around him turned to see what Ashby was looking at.

Trapped on the escalator, Jane and Marsh were suddenly the centre of attention. Cameras flashed as she was recognised. They had no choice but to carry on descending, slowly to the ground floor. She felt Marsh's hand close around hers, letting her know he was there.

At the bottom of the escalator the crowd parted to let them through. They ran a gauntlet of whispering people and flashing cameras until they reached the circle of guards, who, at a word from Ashby, let them through.

'Er . . . Jane,' said Ashby, when she came to a halt directly in front of him. He removed his sunglasses.

She had known him long enough to recognise his nervousness, even though he was trying to look nonchalant in front of his fans. 'Ashby.'

Behind him the band silently nodded their greetings.

Jane linked her arm through Marsh's. 'Marsh, this is Ashby. Ashby, Marshall.'

The two men eyed each other,

unsmiling. Jane remembered Marsh saying that if he ever met her ex, he would punch him on the nose. Her grip on his arm tightened.

Marsh gave her an amused glance and thrust out his hand. 'Pleased to meet you.' His smile didn't match the expression in his eyes. 'I've heard a lot about you.'

Ashby smiled back, employing the full force of his charisma. Several cameras flashed. 'Ladies and gentlemen,' he said with a flourish. 'The lovely Jane and her new partner, Marshall.'

Jane smiled and waved to the crowd, hoping she looked gracious. Marsh waved too, but didn't take his eyes off Ashby.

'Anyway, babe. I've got to go sign some CDs and things. Best of luck to you both.' He caught Marsh's hand for another shake before leaning in to give Jane a swift kiss on the cheek. 'No hard feelings, eh?' he muttered in her ear.

Jane was torn between annoyance

and amusement. How like Ashby. Irritating and enchanting at the same time.

'Right then.' Ashby turned away and strode into the store. 'Somebody give me a pen and let's sign some shit.'

The noise level went up a pitch as the fans forgot all about the newcomers and surged towards their idol. Jane and Marsh, forgotten, shouldered their way through the crowd towards the exit.

'So that was Ashby,' said Marsh, when they reached the street. 'Interesting character.'

'Yeah,' said Jane. 'Irritating as hell.'

'Hmm,' said Marsh. There was a sudden spike in volume from inside. 'They seem to like him.'

'They're welcome to him. I'd much rather have *you*.'

'Likewise.' Marsh put his arm around her waist and together they walked down the street, away from the screaming teenagers.

Jane leaned against him. She felt safe and secure and, for the first time in ages, she realised she was no longer bothered by Ashby. She had Marsh now. He was all she needed.

We do hope that you have enjoyed reading this large print book.

Did you know that all of our titles are available for purchase?

We publish a wide range of high quality large print books including:
Romances, Mysteries, Classics
General Fiction
Non Fiction and Westerns

Special interest titles available in large print are:
The Little Oxford Dictionary
Music Book, Song Book
Hymn Book, Service Book

Also available from us courtesy of Oxford University Press:
Young Readers' Dictionary
(large print edition)
Young Readers' Thesaurus
(large print edition)

For further information or a free brochure, please contact us at:
Ulverscroft Large Print Books Ltd.,
The Green, Bradgate Road, Anstey,
Leicester, LE7 7FU, England.
Tel: (00 44) **0116 236 4325**
Fax: (00 44) **0116 234 0205**